Diana's Pool

A Mystery

Diana K. Perkins

Disclaimer: This is a fictional novel. Any resemblance to actual lives or persons is purely accidental and should not be taken as fact. Although this novel is set in Chaplin, Connecticut, and is based on a local legend, the story is fictional. Some of the buildings, businesses, churches and roads referred to are actual structures and institutions; this is only to create a realistic setting for the novel.

Author's Note: After researching and finding no factual evidence of the legend of Diana's Pool, I felt it was fair to write a fictional account of the possible events leading up to its naming. The true story behind the legend has not surfaced. I would be grateful to hear from anyone with evidence as to why the lovely area on the Natchaug River in Chaplin, Connecticut is called Diana's Pool.

Produced by:
Shetucket Hollow Press
1 Shetucket Drive, Windham, CT 06280-1530
Author's Website: http://www.dianakperkins.com

Acknowledgements

I want to thank my faithful readers who helped and supported me in bringing this novel to fruition: Michelle Giffin, Laura Lawrence, and Christine Pattee, and a special thank you to Terry Cote.

Thank you to my talented editor, Blanche Boucher, who has dedicated many hours to supporting me in my projects.

Thank you to those who helped in the research: the Chaplin Senior Center, Chaplin Historical Society president Marvin Cox, longtime Chaplin residents Warren and Peggy Church, and former Chaplin first selectman Rusty Lanzit.

Thank you to Harrison Judd for the cover photograph. Harrison Judd's website: http://www.futurehistory.com/.

Diana K. Perkins

Dedicated to

My family,

who help bring legends to life

Diana K. Perkins

Chaplin Village, 1935

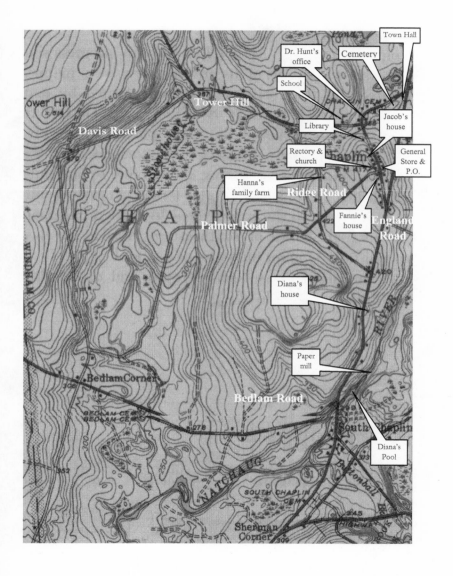

Diana K. Perkins

Chapter 1 – The Funeral

The church is crowded and smells of wet wool and mothballs. The tall windows are letting in a chilly, dull grey light. Everyone is somber, but the low hum of neighbors murmuring gossip fills the silence as we wait for the pastor and casket to come in. I am sitting towards the back of the church with my family. Fannie arrives and motions for me to move closer to the front. My mother nods in assent.

A loud bang echoing through the church signals that the doors have closed, and everyone looks to the back of the church to see who has arrived. Mr. and Mrs. Turner have just come in with their son Jeffrey following.

Mrs. Turner, wearing her hat so low her eyes are nearly obscured, leans into her husband, who pulls her close with his good arm. She has a handkerchief over her mouth that she raises to her eyes as Mr. Turner guides his tear-blinded wife down the aisle. Once the Turners are settled in the front pew, the door bangs again and six mill-worker friends of Mr. Turner bear the casket solemnly down the center aisle, followed by the pastor. The organist starts up a hymn loudly and slightly off-key, but recovers and the music bellows out. The pastor's eyes flick between the open Bible in his hand and the casket as it's placed on the stand. Satisfied that it is set just right and the pallbearers are arranged in the second pew, the pastor pauses by the casket, bowing his head in a short silent prayer, and walks solemnly around it and up to the pulpit.

"Diana was a good girl." He starts with a low voice and the congregation hushes to hear his every word. "How can we not all be touched when a young woman from our own congregation is struck down in her youth?" A murmur of assent rises from the congregation. "I know that some of you," he continues a little louder, "are suspicious of the circumstances." He pauses again and another murmur begins. "But I'm telling you this was an accident!" Focusing on someone who is whispering, he declares loudly, "I knew this girl, and she would not, I repeat,"—he pauses—"would not take her own life." He looks out across the congregation, waiting for someone to move or talk, but there is total silence, all eyes on either him or the casket. Mrs. Turner stifles a sob. All of us are struck by the pastor's direct approach to what has already caused gossip and has been an engrossing topic in our small town.

The pastor continues. "I could not in good conscience speak to you or bury this poor soul in the Church if I had any doubt as to the cause. This was an accident. Let her rest in peace." A low murmur starts up again and he looks sternly out across his flock. "Diana was a kind woman, a good woman, a child still, and we will all miss her and mourn her loss, but she has gone to be with our Father in Heaven." He bows his head. "I will now read from Ecclesiastes 3:1." As his words flow people crane to see Mrs. Turner, who is now sobbing openly.

The pastor instructs us to sing the hymn Amazing Grace, and then asks us to say the Lord's Prayer with him. Then he invites us all to join the family after the burial in the church meeting room, where volunteers have set up a potluck buffet.

Waiting for the casket to be carried out we hear Mrs. Turner sobbing again, and as she starts to walk up the aisle behind the casket, she pauses, turns, and points directly at me, shaking her head.

I am mortified. I try to make myself small, hiding behind the shoulder of my school chum Fannie who stands next to me. All the people who have seen Mrs. Turner's gesture turn to fix on me as I bow my head and try not to look at anyone. I clasp my hands, squeeze my eyes tight and pretend to be silently praying. Mrs. Turner, urged by her husband, turns back towards the aisle, and they resume their slow walk behind the casket. The pastor follows, and those from the pews closest to the front queue out after them. I'm chilled but sweating. Fannie jabs me with her elbow and whispers to me, "Don't worry, she is just crazed by grief." We all file slowly out of the church, down the steps and up the road. The casket has been placed on a dressed-up hay wagon harnessed to an old dray with his winter coat filling in. One of the men grasps the bridle and leads the horse and wagon to the cemetery, which is only seven or eight houses down the road. We walk silently in the chilly air. It's cold enough to see our breath. Dry leaves scatter in the light breeze. The only sounds are the horse clomping slowly and the wooden wagon wheels and feet crunching on the pavement and leaves. A blue jay screeches. I'm wondering how I could sneak out and run back home without being noticed, but it's impossible; people turn now and then to look at me.

For a while no one speaks, and then someone breaks the silence with small talk about the early autumn. I look out at the grays and browns of this swiftly closing season, thinking how appropriate this task is to the dreary day. I hang far back in the procession, and when we stop I stay in the back of the group that gathers around the open grave. The grave has only two boards across it to hold the casket above the dark hole. A few people put a rose on the casket, and someone else steps forward with a bunch of asters.

The pastor waits until everyone has gathered and then starts to pray, his voice rising above the breeze that has now picked up. I am not comforted by his words. I am angry. I have lost my friend and my confidant and she is not coming back. Will we meet in the next life as he is claiming? It is a weak offering to those of us who are left behind. I stare at the casket and the hole below it, imagining what it must be like to be at the bottom with dirt thrown in upon me. I'm roused from my morbid thoughts by the eerie feeling that someone is watching me, and when I look up I meet Jacob Sparks's stare. He looks quickly away, but as I keep my eyes on him he looks back and gives me a weak smile.

Jacob was her boyfriend. Why wasn't Mrs. Turner pointing at him and shaking her head? The Turners didn't really give their permission, but Diana and Jacob had been spending time together. The Turners actually hadn't seemed to mind either way. After school Jacob would walk her home. While at school they would eat lunch together in a remote corner of the large room that served as a cafeteria. The Sparkses hadn't approved of Jacob's interest in Diana, and they'd tried to thwart the alliance. They were in church this morning but stayed far to the back, and chose not to go to the cemetery. I saw them turning up the sidewalk to their fine home on the way. They waved Jacob to go home with them but he ignored them and followed the procession to the grave. Their other two sons did not bother to attend.

I hardly knew Jacob; I had seen him only on the walk home from school. The crowd of students thinned as we passed their homes, till only a few of us remained. Diana and Fannie and I lived the farthest away, and Jacob, whose house we had already passed, began walking us all to the end. The turn-off to my road was before the others so Diana told me all that had happened in the last months. That he had often followed her as they walked home from school, finally walked next to her, and later carried her books. Gradually they had become friends, but Diana knew that his parents didn't like her; they did not try to keep it a secret. When she saw them at the post office or the market they seemed to try to avoid her, and if caught face to face made the barest acknowledgment of her. For her part, she was embarrassed by their actions, which made her feel cheap and poor, "like she was" she said. They knew and she knew. So she didn't understand Jacob's attraction to her. Was it an effort to go against his parents? Was it because she might be easier than the more well-to-do girls? She didn't speak these thoughts to him. She just watched him, trying to see the crack in the sincere friendship he offered her. But she told me. She told it all to me. From what I could see, Jacob *was* sincere, and I told her so. He didn't try to become friendly with me or with any other girls. He was polite to me but nothing more. She did not enlist me to watch him, but when she voiced her concern I told her the truth. I told her what I saw. He is a good-hearted boy, I told her, not the scholar that his brothers were but good enough. Not an athlete, but not a wimp either. He would make a good husband, I teased, and she'd shush me. We all wanted a husband, a good husband, but we also wanted a marriage that would last, and if there was a big difference in our social status, well, that marriage might not last. Of course a Prince Charming would be wonderful, but it would likely work only if you were a princess in disguise.

So here I am, looking across this far-too-early grave into the pained eyes of Diana's boyfriend Jacob. I look away, but when I look back he is still gazing at me. I make a quick scan of the crowd to see if anyone is watching us. When I look at him again he mouths some words at me, but I don't understand them. I just raise my shoulders in a gesture that says, "I don't know." I don't want to get caught up in an exchange with him, I want to escape, to go home and hide in my room and be left alone. Fannie maneuvers behind a small group and slowly eases in next to me, in a whisper asking to sit with me when we go back to the church. I nod yes, grateful to be saved from other interactions with Jacob. The pastor says a final word and we all turn back towards the road. I am now near the front of the group and I hang back to let others pass, watching the man leading the empty wagon back towards the road. The Turners remain by the grave looking mournfully down at the casket. Mr. Anders, one of our schoolteachers, also lingers, one arm around the waist of his wife, the other wiping his eyes with a handkerchief. We are all still in shock. Our community is finding it hard to believe this still-very-fresh tragedy.

In the church basement tables set up along one side are laden with pots of soup, bowls of salad, baskets of biscuits, urns of coffee and plates of the sweeter offerings. My mother gives me a plate of cookies to set out and I squeeze between the other women who are arranging the buffet. Long tables in the center are set up with chairs, and people have already laid claim to spots. Others are filling in the open spaces, looking to find a seat near friends or family.

Fannie, who at the gravesite asked to sit near me, has several seats saved, and she motions furtively to me. I slowly shoulder my way through the quickly-filling room and leave my coat on the empty chair next to hers. As I do, several of our other girlfriends join us. I can see Jacob edging his way towards us until someone takes his arm and points him to a spot adjacent to them. We are mostly all seated when the pastor and the Turners come in. They sit near the front of the hall. The pastor stands and motions for us all to do so. He speaks a few words, blessing the food and saying that it is a sad occasion to be gathering together but that Diana will be dining with a far more heavenly crowd today as Jesus and his Father have prepared a banquet for her. For a moment I bow my head with the others, but then I raise it slightly to look around. The mourners stand with hands clasped in prayer, heads bowed and eyes closed, with only an occasional curious eye peeking like mine. A sniffle here and a cough there, and then the pastor blesses us and turns to escort the Turners to the buffet. Everyone watches in silence. Mrs. Turner takes just a few small helpings, and her husband at her elbow ushers her back across the room. Once the Turners are seated a line starts at the beginning of the buffet. As people proceed through and sit down to eat, conversation starts to fill the silence and the volume grows. People go back and approach the dessert table and then get a cup of coffee. They linger in their seats talking quietly; an occasional louder laugh makes some turn to look at the disrupter. No one is rushing off. On such a dreary day nobody is in a hurry to go home.

Fannie and the other girls sitting with me are bursting with questions but polite enough not to ask them. I am sad, and barely eating. I focus on my plate as I see them glance surreptitiously at me. Fannie, sitting beside me, jabs me in the side with her elbow and mutters, "Don't look. Jacob is heading this way." I sink lower into my seat, now leaning on my arm with my hand shading my eyes. I poke at the food with my fork. I see the girls part to let him near me and then see his feet under my shaded eyes as he presses close and taps me on the shoulder. Even though I know he's there, I start before I turn to look at him. I feel everyone is watching.

Jacob bends down and whispers to me, "Hanna, I've got to talk to you." I shake my head no. "I know you were there and I have to talk to you." I look up at him and we hold each other's eyes for a few seconds. I nod. He bends down to whisper in my ear again. "Monday, after school, meet me on the corner." I nod. He straightens up, gives the others an acknowledging wave and turns to head out the door.

All the girls look at me as I again lower my gaze to my plate. Fannie pokes me and says, "Come on, let's get out of here." We all rise to leave. I feel like everyone is still watching me and I hurry out the door. I take a deep breath of the cold fresh air and sigh out the little cloud of steam. Fannie hooks her arm in mine and starts talking to fill the silence. "Why is he bugging you? You didn't do anything."

Fannie, who is almost as good as Diana at understanding my moods, tries to cheer me up. She starts by talking about the boys who were there and the families she thinks are hypocrites because she imagines they went only to see the grief of others. I walk along silently, with only nods to her declarations. Finally we reach the turn-off to my home and I tell her I'll see her in school on Monday. I wave her off and slowly walk up the road.

As I approach my house I study the windows. I know my family will be inside, likely talking about the morning, and won't give me a moment's peace. And I need some solace. I stand there for some minutes. I'm agitated, wondering what to do. What does Jacob know? Are my imaginings, which sometimes run away with me, causing my distress? No, I'm afraid he knows. Really knows. But it wasn't my fault. I have to keep repeating that to myself so I will believe it. It wasn't my fault.

It's cold. I head towards the house and at every step I repeat, "It wasn't my fault, it wasn't my fault, it wasn't my fault," until I arrive at my door, go in, and am greeted with warmth, cooking smells and the shouts of my brother and younger sister bickering. It wasn't my fault.

Chapter 2 - Chaplin

I grew up in this small town of Chaplin, where my family has a farm just outside the village. Everyone knows us and we know everyone. It's average as small towns go. It has a post office and general store, a tavern and a couple of small businesses. Our elementary school history classes included the settlement of Chaplin. We learned that a Benjamin Chaplin settled the little town. Rather than the town growing up around a factory as many did, we incorporated as an ecclesiastical society. Then mills opened on the proud waters of the Natchaug River: a saw mill, a grist mill, a paper mill and others. Still we were principally a farming town.

The beautiful Natchaug River that runs through town is enjoyed for recreation too. On warm summer days not only do the children frolic in its swirling pools but women often picnic on the shores while their husbands fish for a trout supper.

Our main street is a sweet lane of lovely homes, some imposing, some modest, but most well-maintained. A few of the families have been in the town since its incorporation.

Our new library is a handsome building with a turret and lots of room for many shelves of books. It was built on the main street and is within close walking distance for most of us.

Although I feel lucky to be living and growing up in this little town, I also feel the constraints and the pressures of conformity that come along with it. What will my future bring? Will I be a farm wife like my mother? Will I be a teacher, or will I move to a city and find employment as a secretary? My future is open, but limited. If I were a man I would have no limitations. I am smart and industrious; I could be anything. But I am a woman.

I have always been a bit envious of Diana. But look at what has become of her. Some said she was a character, some said an odd girl; some said she was dangerous and some even called her evil, crossing their fingers and muttering "Witch." But she was none of these. She was my friend and a free spirit, a soul not stamped from the general Chaplin die. A small town like this doesn't usually like people who are different. It wants people to be like them, to look like them and to act like them. Threats to its closed society can be measured in those wagging tongues. It wants people it can understand, not an untamed girl who reads Tarot cards. It was this wildness, this carefree mindset that I envied. While the rest of us were conforming to the narrow vision of the town Diana was on her own path.

That path led to her death and shook the town. Those who hadn't liked her were afraid she might come back to take revenge. Those who knew her could not understand what had happened. The town was polarized and everyone was trying to come to a measure of resolution.

I for one felt her loss was the fault of someone in the town, and if possible I was going to find out who and why.

Chapter 3 – Jacob

All day long at school on Monday, knowing that I am to meet Jacob later, I am nervous to the point of almost being ill. Fannie and a few others meet me for lunch and we gossip and talk about our classes. This small talk is a welcome diversion and I am more relaxed for the rest of the day until the time comes for school dismissal. Now I am again nervous.

Fannie and I leave school together. Diana often joined us on the walk home. Today the walk without her is oddly solemn. Before Fannie turns off towards her house we hug, an acknowledgement of the loss we're feeling. I go up the road that will bring me closer to home. The next corner, under an ancient oak, is where we would all meet if we were walking to the library or just to visit. This is the turn-off to my house. I can see Jacob standing there, looking somber. I am a bundle of nerves. He catches sight of me and nods as I approach, and rather than turn down the road to my house we continue up the hill. Without speaking we understand our common desire to be discreet. Jacob offers to carry my books but I have only one and tell him it is not heavy. After a few minutes of walking in silence he begins. "Did *you* find her?" I am startled that he is so direct.

"I'm sorry," he continues. "I need to talk about this. I need to understand. Can we? Can you talk about it?" I nod and we continue walking up the hill. I hesitate, but then begin to recite the event that has played over and over in my mind.

"It was Sunday evening. I knew she was distressed. I had seen her at church that morning and she was upset; she was crying. I asked her why, what the matter was, but she just shook her head and shrugged, agitated, and finally left the service before it was over." I look sideways at Jacob and he nods, motioning for me to continue. "I knew she was troubled. I just did not know why, not for sure. Earlier in the week she had said something about you. I was surprised. She thought you were losing interest or that there was someone else..." I look at him again.

He stops, also surprised. "Losing interest? Someone else? Where did she get that?"

"I don't know. She just mentioned it in passing. She seemed so agitated that I didn't get a chance to ask more. I wasn't able to get to see her again until late that day. In the afternoon I walked to her house but she wasn't home. Her mother said she was meeting me. I was surprised because we hadn't made plans. So I walked to the library, then through the center of town to the school, thinking I would see her on the way. When I didn't find her I wasn't sure where to go. I went back home, passing the corner where we usually met, that one back there where you and I just met. But she wasn't there. She wasn't anywhere." I point back from where we just came, then continue. "I went back out. By then the sun was setting and it would start to get dark soon. I went back past her house. I peered in to see if she was home yet but I didn't see her. Then I went to the bridge. It was the last place I could think of. I thought maybe she had gone to the pool. Then I saw her in the water." I am speaking fast and I start to cry. "It was her dress. I could see her dress in the pool, caught on a rock as the water rushed around it. I think I screamed her name. I rushed over to her. She was under the water. I grabbed her arm and pulled her out. It was hard because the water dragged on her and I slipped several times and thought I would fall in with her."

I pause. Jacob is looking intensely at me. He takes hold of my arm and urges, "And then what?"

"She was cold, shockingly cold, and a blue-white color." I start to sob. "I thought, she's dead. I pulled her up onto the rocks where the water couldn't reach her and then I screamed, 'Help! Help!' and ran back to the Turners' house." Jacob still has my arm but he is looking away distractedly. Then he turns back to me.

"Then what?"

"I tell Mrs. Turner and she yells to her husband and we all run back to the pool. Her brother is sent to the neighbors to call for help. We run back, but she is still there, lying as I have left her, not moving, not breathing."

Jacob releases my arm. "So, do you think that is why Mrs. Turner pointed at you?"

"I imagine she thinks it is my fault, that I was supposed to be with her, but I didn't know that. She started screaming at me, asking me what happened. I told her I didn't know but she couldn't stop crying and screaming. Mr. Turner held Diana, just sitting on the rocks cradling her and petting her cold wet hair. Then the constable and several others arrived. The constable sent me home and came later to talk to me, but that was the last I saw of Diana. I didn't even get to say goodbye."

Jacob turns and faces me. "What do you think happened?"

I shake my head. "I don't know. I only know she was acting strangely, out of character. Maybe she was by the rocks and something frightened her or she slipped. You know she frequently walked down there and sat by the water. She loved the pools and how pretty it was there. She said it didn't matter what season, that it was always a beautiful sight. You could hear the river from her bedroom window. You could hear the water rushing over the rocks from pool to pool. She loved that, listening to it at night. She told me that sometimes she'd sneak out late at night when everyone else was asleep and go down to the river." Jacob nods as if he knows this, as if she had told him too.

He interrupts me. "She wasn't breathing?"

"No, she wasn't breathing or moving at all."

21

"She was cold?"

"Yes. I was shocked at how cold she was."

Jacob starts to sob. I don't know what to do. I try to soothe him, putting an arm over his shoulder, but he pushes me away, turns and strides a few feet, bends over and sobs again. I can only stand there watching, feeling helpless. He finally pulls out his handkerchief and blows his nose, wipes his eyes, and turns back to me.

"Sorry."

"It's okay."

"I loved her, you know."

"Yes."

"I never told her. Now I can't."

"I think that wherever she is, she knows that you loved her. We used to talk together and she said she thought you were an Adonis, that you were so handsome. I think she knew you loved her."

"It's insane." Jacob's tone is rising. "We're talking about her in the past tense. It's impossible! How can this be? How can she be gone?" His face is a grotesque mask of grief. I can only shake my head and say, "I don't understand it either."

By now we've walked a mile up the hill, past my turn-off. "I need to get back." Jacob nods and we turn around.

"My parents didn't like her. You knew that, didn't you? I think everyone did. They said I could do better, that she was beneath me." He repeated, "Beneath me. She knew, and it hurt her. I think that's why she tried to keep me at a distance. She probably knew they would have made it very difficult for us."

"Yes, they probably would have." I can't disagree.

"My brothers didn't care one way or the other about her except they thought I should 'have more fun with other girls' like they did. They don't take any girls seriously. They just use them, and when the girls get too attached they break it off. I hate the way they are with girls." I nod again. I've heard rumors about how his brothers jilt their girlfriends, and now that they are in college I am sure they are still doing it. Like their father, they have little respect for women.

"How are your brothers doing?" I think I should ask.

"Oh, they're good. They just went back to school. They had been on break but even when they're in school they come home a lot. My mother loves it when they're home. She says her family is complete again. She spoils them and they fawn over her. It almost makes me sick because I know they don't respect her." Suddenly Jacob realizes how open he is being with me. "Oh, sorry. This is really nothing that has to do with you."

"I understand. I know how families can be." I feel a small corner has been turned. A new level of friendship is growing between us; we have a common bond.

We're nearing the turn-off to my house, and I can sense a growing urgency in his manner. "You don't think it was an accident, do you?"

We stop under the oak and I turn to look straight at him. "No."

"Please meet with me again, will you? I want to find out what happened."

"Okay, but I can't until next week, and you know I'm not supposed to be talking about this. The constable told me not to. He said they were still 'investigating' it. I don't want to get into trouble, or give away any information that I'm not supposed to, but I told all this to him. So you must promise not to tell anyone that I've told you this. Do you swear?"

"Yes, it is just between us. I promise." Jacob nods seriously. "If it wasn't an accident, we will be the best people to figure out what happened."

I nod back at him. "See you next Friday? Right here?" He nods again.

"In the meantime let's keep our senses keen and watch and listen. Someone may give us a clue."

In a spontaneous act of bonding I hug him, and he hugs me back; then I turn swiftly and walk briskly home. I don't look back but I sense he is watching me.

This has given me much to think about. I needn't have been nervous.

When I arrive home my younger sister greets me with a running hug and I drop my book to swing her around.

"Hanna!" she screams, "Where have you been? I've been waiting for hours for you to get home and help me with the cream."

Then from the kitchen my mother speaks loudly enough for me to hear. "Hanna, why do you dilly-dally so? We need your help here. Will you please come into the kitchen and help Amy skim the cream?"

"Yes. Sorry. Coming." I rush upstairs and change out of my school clothes and into ones I can get dirty. I go downstairs to wash my hands and don my apron. Amy and I use the skimmers to gently skim the layer of cream off the large pan of milk.

"Okay, Mom, we're done. Do you want us to make some of it into butter?"

"Let Amy do that. You go do your homework."

I smile at Mom and kiss my little sister on the forehead. She sticks her tongue out at me. "Careful. You'll lose that one day," I tease.

I find it hard to focus on my homework but finally finish it. We have supper, clean up and do our evening chores, and then at last I'm able to climb into bed next to the already sleeping Amy, who occasionally wants to sleep with me. All the last week's events start circulating through my mind. Will I get into trouble for telling what I know to Jacob? How would anyone find out?

Will he honor his word and keep my disclosure a secret? Was someone else involved? I didn't see anyone but I was not looking. Once I found her I didn't notice anything else and ran off so quickly that anyone else there had plenty of time to walk out casually. But how could someone do that, murder an innocent girl? Maybe she wasn't innocent. This insane questioning of every aspect of every person, of their character and possible motives, has me wondering if perhaps we are not only chasing shadows and making more of this than there is, but also sacrificing the basic belief in the goodness of people to the sinister suspicions of the worst side of their characters. Do we really want to know? Will we really find something? I am a simple, caring person. What do I know of the evil side, of the dark side? All these thoughts nag at me until I finally fall into a fitful sleep, and I dream of Diana and Jacob and myself, all happily dancing in a field of daisies when a dark cloud suddenly appears and a heavy shower drenches us and leaves us cold and soaked and looking forlornly at each other. I awake with a start, gasping for air as though I'm drowning.

I have a flashing vision of a memory but it quickly dissolves as wakefulness envelops me.

Chapter 4 - Diana

Throughout the next week I try to bring all the memories I've ever had of Diana into my consciousness. I start to make lists of her character traits. I talk to people who knew her, trying to ask discreet questions in the guise of a dear friend wanting to remember her lost companion. All the while I'm looking for clues to her seemingly irrational behavior in the weeks before her death.

Diana was shy but approachable. Once I became her friend I found her open, frank and sincere. Generally kind-hearted, she championed the underdog and was not afraid to intervene when she perceived an injustice. She would sometimes confront bullies and then become the object of abuse herself. She loved animals and went to extremes to try to save injured ones and to protect those that were being treated unfairly. She once freed a dog that had been chained for years and brought it home with her. When the owner found out where the dog was she persuaded him to let her keep it rather than have it chained up in all kinds of weather and never let loose to run. Her parents reluctantly supported the animal welfare child they had raised, but told her they could not afford to have her bringing home any more 'hounds.' People would sometimes bring injured animals to her to nurse. She'd found a crow hatchling and nursed it until it was able to fend for itself and it followed her everywhere, to school and home. She fed Cecil table scraps that weren't appropriate for the dog and cats and Cecil cawed his thanks. Sometimes Cecil sat outside her bedroom window and called to her and occasionally she'd let him in. She would rescue bugs caught in the house, and outdoors she avoided stepping on them. She'd protect snakes from silly boys who tried to kill them.

But it wasn't just animals; it was all living things—the wildflowers that grew so abundantly, the trees that filled her woods. She thought all these things deserved to be protected, that they are made not for us and our use but as part of the earth, and are as sacred as humans. She expressed that opinion several times but after people told her she was not sane or realistic, she started to keep it to herself. She was what some called a 'bleeding heart.' Although these ideals of hers were not the common views, they were not that unusual. Did Diana carry them to the extreme? Maybe, but was that a reason for her dramatic end? Could it have contributed? I think it unlikely.

The Turners were not regular church-goers. They had started attending the Congregational church in the town center, but once the children had gotten a little older they stopped going regularly and finally stopped altogether. Diana was not compelled to attend church, nor did she find it fulfilling. When she went to the Catholic church with a friend from Willimantic, she was inspired. It was awesome, not austere. It was grand, not plain. It felt spiritual, not dogmatic. Even though she didn't understand what was happening because the Mass was said in Latin, she was impressed with the seeming devoutness of the worshipers. She would have liked to go to that church but it was too far away to attend regularly. Instead she started to study the Catholic tradition, reading the Catholic Bible and acquiring a Catholic missal. She found a step-stool out in the back shed and covered it with a towel and a piece of green cloth to make it look like a prayer kneeler. She begged a crucifix from her Catholic friend and nailed it up on the wall in the corner of her tiny room. On a handkerchief beneath the crucifix she set a candle in a jar in front her makeshift prie-dieu[1]. She would kneel and say her morning and evening prayers in Latin as they were shown in the missal. Someone gave her a medal of the Blessed Virgin Mary that she

---

[1] A desk-like kneeling bench used for praying.

wore beneath her blouse day and night. Mostly her parents ignored this, but once when her mother peeked in and saw the lit candle and Diana on her knees chanting strange Latin prayers, she mentioned it to her father, who asked her if she was going to become a nun. She was embarrassed by the inquiry. Someone had intruded on her private prayers and somehow made them seem silly.

Gradually she moved away from her attachment to the Catholic faith, but then became enamored of the Jewish faith. This was more difficult. She could study it but since she wasn't Jewish by blood, entering into that faith would be very difficult. Still she read about their ceremonies and traditions. She used a winter scarf as a prayer shawl and nailed a small tin to her bedroom door jamb as a mezuzah. She inquired amongst her Jewish classmates, politely asking as much as she could. But finally she realized that without a teacher she likely would never learn Hebrew or read a Torah.

None of these or other faiths she'd read about filled her spiritual needs. She delved into the darker arts, drawing an upside-down pentagram on a wooden box, where she kept a black candle and a black cloth, some quartz crystals, a small dagger, and a skunk's skull she had once found. She had no idea what she was doing or what kind of spells her attempts at incantations might cast. For several months she wore a black mantilla to school and would look mysteriously out from under its lowered veil. People thought she had lost her mind, but it was just Diana trying out her personal expression of freedom. She was a wild and yet very conservative young girl, and all the jeers and pressures to conform that she contended with only served to make her stronger and more independent. Some of the people in school made fun of her, others gossiped about her, and some were afraid of her and thought she might truly have powers that they didn't understand. Could she have made enemies because of her curiosity? Would someone who held their faith dear go to an extreme to defend it? Would someone feel she was evil or delving into dangerous territory when she read about black magic? Did she bring it upon herself in some strange twist of the supernatural? I hope to find out.

I knew her as not only a friend but as a smart and creative person. She could draw and sew and play the piano without having taken lessons. She seemed to know what people were thinking and would use this ability to frighten those who didn't like her. She knew how to interpret dreams and seemed able to predict the future. She taught herself to read Tarot cards. She knew which wild plants were good to eat and which were poisonous. She knew which mushrooms were unsafe. I heard a few people, even adults, mutter the word 'witch.' But both she and I just laughed at that, although I think she secretly liked being an odd person. While it seemed to make her more of an outcast, I could not imagine that people in this century could be so silly as to think she actually was a witch.

I believe she liked me because I was kind to her, but maybe also because I wasn't afraid of her. I kept her secrets and gained her confidence. She had so few people she could confide in that she sought me out more often than was sometimes comfortable for me. When classmates teased me because we were friends I just hushed them, calling them silly ignoramuses. I think I helped to give her a measure of respectability, and in turn she gave me an edge of the unpredictable.

Her unusual interests ebbed and flowed. Sometimes a taste for science or music would eclipse her interest in the less-conventional areas. Handwriting intrigued her, and she once showed me a book on graphology that she was studying; she analyzed my handwriting with frightening accuracy. She decided to learn German, then French, never getting further than a few short phrases before she moved on to something else. But she always remained true to her love of animals and the natural world; that stayed with her.

Some of her classmates liked her and some avoided her. Since she wasn't in one of the cliques she felt the freedom to be an individual. Most boys were not interested. Diana was not a beauty. She was attractive but was starting to get acne, which made her more sensitive and insecure. She was strong, athletic and, for most of her teen years, flat-chested. She kept her fine, mousy-brown hair short so that it didn't interfere with any of her outdoor adventures. Her long walks in the woods or along the river being dragged by a large dog on a leash kept her in shape, and so I think she would have been strong enough to swim.

She didn't seem to care about boys until she reached sixteen. Then she hoped they would be interested. At that age many of the boys were looking at her in a different way: this was not just the quirky girl of yore, but a strange and interesting woman. Most were too insecure to imagine having her as a girlfriend. They feared not only her independent spirit but also the jibes of the other boys. Only Jacob could see her softer side. He saw her kindness and caring for animals, which he shared. Jacob was shy too, and for months he stayed behind us on his way home. Finally one day he caught up and asked if he could walk with us. Still, he was silent and just listened to our banter. We were not sure why he chose to walk with us. Was he interested in one of us? Was it Fannie or Diana or me? When he reached his house he'd turn and climb the steps and go in. Eventually he would walk past his house and as each of us turned off to go home, he continued to walk Diana to the end of the village, and then went back to his house. They grew to be good friends, walking in the woods and along the river, throwing stones for the dog to chase and picking wildflowers.

Both Jacob and I learned more about Diana's home life during these long walks home from school. Her father worked at the paper mill situated at a dam on the Natchaug River below their home. The mill made paper for newsprint. Jacob's father worked there too, but having more education than most he quickly rose to a managerial position. Diana's father, Ephraim, ran the machines that made the pulpwood. Years ago he was injured at the mill and lost the use of one of his arms, which now dangled uselessly. He sometimes said he wished it had just been amputated. After the accident he would occasionally buy a bottle of liquor, and go on a bender, losing his temper and throwing things around. Everyone knew to stay clear when he was in a snit, and at these times Diana would usually go for a long walk. Sitting by the river and listening to the water falling over the rocks calmed her, and by the time she got back to the house her father had quieted down. She said he was a good man and had been a hard worker. But work at the mill didn't pay that well, and they always seemed to be barely scraping by and sometimes even in debt. He was always fearful that in a downturn the mill would let him go. Because he had been so long at the mill he couldn't understand why with such a steady job they couldn't do better. Her older brother Jeffrey, although Diana thought him lazy, was a vigorous young man and able to do the things around the house that her father found too difficult: splitting wood, shoveling snow, mowing the tiny lawn and helping their mother with the small garden.

Diana's mother, Anna, tried to pick up odd jobs when she could. She would do housekeeping and sewing and even take in laundry—whatever would give them a little extra cash. They lived close to the village and her jobs at the nicer homes were a simple ten-minute walk for her. She was a happy woman even though times were tough for the family. She always greeted people with a bright smile and would chuckle with everyone at off-color jokes. She whistled while she hung out the clothes and while she cooked. People liked her and her honest, easy-going ways, and she gained the trust of the families she worked for.

During the past summer, before it all went wrong, Diana had started working at the mill. She was happy to get the job and could help out with bills and also have a little extra money for food and supplies for her animals. Not only did she have the dog, she also fed three or four cats that hung around the house and she would buy food for any other wild thing that needed help. She was able to get Cecil the crow some special treats. Cecil hung around the back door on the lower limbs of the maple that grew there. Diana would step out and Cecil would fly to the ground and hop around looking sideways at her, waiting for the bits of bread or the bologna she was sometimes able to afford. Cecil loved bologna, which he'd hold with his feet and pull apart in strips before gobbling it down.

Her parents were grateful that her job allowed her to help with rent. She said the only fly in the ointment was Mr. Sparks, who wanted nothing more than to make this a lesson in why women shouldn't be doing men's work and why she, a menial worker, shouldn't be dating the boss's son. It was all silly to her. She could move pulp around; it wasn't that difficult. And as far as she was concerned she wasn't really dating Jacob; they were just friends. While Mr. Sparks never directly told her how he felt, she got the message. Other workers were told to assign her menial jobs, so she would have to stop her regular work and clean out the bathroom or help a particularly mean fellow who didn't like having women employed in the mill. Her father, who was usually working in other parts of the mill, didn't see the indirect attacks. If her brother did he thought them justified or too petty to be of concern. Diana, though, did not say anything. She just did her work and the additional tasks without comment, as if it were the most natural thing in the world to be treated so unfairly.

But she talked about it to me, saying how she hoped for revenge one day, and she would secretly chant curses over a cigarette she saw Mr. Sparks throw down on his way home. She said it had his aura on it and she would send his soul to a dark place and his body into the mill sluice. For all of her outward boldness she also knew when she should go along with the flow of either events or people. This made her a shrewd and dangerous adversary.

Other than the difficulties at the mill Diana thought she had a good life. The expectation was that she would probably find herself a nice millworker or farmer for a husband, settle down and have a family. That she hadn't figured out what she wanted did not trouble her family. Everyone knew there was no money for any higher education. She was smart and clever but not a great student other than in biology. Any dreams she had of being something more than a housewife were impossibilities, and besides, she couldn't alight on any one dream long enough to put real energy into it.

Now that she was seventeen her body was maturing even more. Finally breasts were forming and body hair was emerging, and an intense energy and excitement were driving her. Desires that she was embarrassed to discuss with her mother were occasional topics that she and I approached cautiously. She shyly asked me questions. Did I ever kiss a boy? What did it feel like? Was it exciting? Did I ever go any further than that? I trusted her so I answered her, but I was no more experienced than she. A few times one of my brothers had tried to touch my breasts but I'd smacked him. It seemed okay if we accidentally touched each other when we were little and we were wrestling, but as we got older those boundaries were drawn and I understood them and made sure my brothers did too. I wondered if Diana had those kinds of issues with her brother, but she never approached the subject. I thought if she had she might have been too embarrassed to talk about it.

Classmates told me what they could remember but only rarely did they tell me something I didn't already know. Diana and I shared so much of our personal lives that I can't imagine what could have happened to drive her down to the river. Was it an accident or was it deliberate? I try to imagine what could possibly be the cause.

Chapter 5 – Our Families

Jacob and I meet again the next Friday. It has become colder so we decide to move to the library, which is convenient and on the way to our homes.

The librarian looks at us curiously. In this small town everyone knows everyone else and most know one another's business. They gossip about what they do know, or speculate in creative ways about what they don't. We realize this will seem suspicious to the librarian, especially since we had been friends with Diana, but we sit down at a table near the curved front windows as far from prying eyes and ears as we can manage. We open our school books and make it look as though we are doing homework together.

"Did you find out anything?" Jacob begins, looking intently across the book at me, pencil in hand, ready to take notes.

"Not much we didn't already know," is my simple reply, and he puts his pencil to paper, looking studious.

"Well, I didn't get much either, not yet, but we need to be persistent."

I nod. "My sister said she'd heard some rumor about a boy who had been picking on Diana in class. Diana didn't mention it to me. I think it was her biology class, where she was actually one of the top students. She loved science classes, unlike math and English classes. Grace–you know my older sister Grace?–said she thought this guy had a crush on Diana. Grace had to make up this class; otherwise she wouldn't have been in it with Diana. So anyway, she thought it was odd, the way he singled her out and teased her. Grace didn't understand whether the guy liked her or didn't like her."

"When was this? Did she tell you?" Jacob seems interested in this new information.

"It began just this year, right after classes started." Seeing from the corner of my eye that the librarian is passing the doorway, I pause to look down at my book and turn the page. "She said he would make fun of her. Diana was the first to raise her hand when the teacher asked a question, and this boy would mutter in a loud whisper that others could hear, something like 'know-it-all' and similar things. She said Diana usually ignored him except this one time when she confronted him and told him he was going to lose the use of his tongue if he didn't shut up. And he did shut up. He didn't make a peep after that."

"Did Grace give you a name?" Jacob probes.

"No. I'll ask her, but she did say he was very upset by Diana's death. He even missed a couple days of school right after it happened."

"What about your other sisters? Did you ask them?"

"Ida—you know, Grace's twin? I asked her, but she didn't have too much to say. She doesn't seem to pay much attention to the younger set, and that's how she sees us, pretty much as kids. My younger sister and my brothers didn't have much to say either since they seem preoccupied with the younger people much as Ida is with the older people. Amy and Nathaniel would see her when they walked to their piano lessons. They said she'd often be walking on the roadside or in the woods, dressed in rough clothes, almost like a man. When they saw her like that they thought she was weird." I stop and look absently at the book open before me, turning the page before I continue. "When she came to our house for supper, as she did often, she was dressed in her school clothes, so she didn't look so out of place. Everyone thought she was pleasant and polite. These were the times when she seemed most normal. My parents liked her, and knowing her circumstances they often sent her home with milk or eggs. At those times she seemed like any other friend of ours, but I could see a strain and thought she was uncomfortable and making an effort to fit in."

Jacob is nodding as I talk, agreeing with what I am saying. "Yes, I'd seen her walking through the woods with those rough trousers on. She could look odd, but also oddly alluring." Realizing this is perhaps an admission he shouldn't have made, he quickly switches his gaze from the book to me. I watch his face go through a transformation from an almost pleasant half-smile to surprise and then to guilt. "Oh, I don't mean that I was thinking about her *that* way. I just liked the freedom it seemed to give her. It seemed to suit her independent spirit." He is almost pleading for me to understand. I nod. I know what he meant. "Don't worry. I understand."

He becomes business-like. "Did your family say anything else?"

I shake my head. "No. I didn't have a lot of time to talk to them about her. You know we run a busy farm and we always have chores. I'd fit questions in privately when I could, and I didn't want to arouse any suspicion either." I turn another page. "After it first happened we talked about it around the dinner table for a couple of days. My family knew we were friends and knew I found her in the river, so all of them were carefully choosing their words, not wanting to upset me. They thought the whole thing curious. They did have opinions about what had happened. Mostly they thought she had an accident on the rocks, but Grace thought maybe she was upset about being jilted. There was talk of that. You know rumors and how they spread." I watch him. "They don't mean anything. No one knew what was going on. They just talk."

He nods. "But none of it is true. I was not seeing anyone else. I was not really even seeing her. I wish people didn't make assumptions. It puts everyone in a bad light."

The librarian walks into the room and up to our table. We start reading our texts.

"How is your *studying* going?" She says this in a stern and almost sarcastic tone.

Both of us answer, "Fine, thank you."

I look up. "We have a history test coming up." I've offered more than is her business. We are fortunate to have a class together and to truly have a test coming up. She turns around and as she goes through the doorway offers over her shoulder, "Good luck." She doesn't sound at all sincere.

Jacob and I look at each other and smile. "Maybe we really should do some studying," I say. "If I don't keep my grades up my parents may pull me out to work on the farm with them." I look down at my book. It is opened to chapters nowhere near the ones I need to study.

"So," I begin again, "what did you find out? Anything from your family?"

"Not very much. My brothers are jerks, you know. They have so little regard for women. I could barely speak of it without them making jokes about her trousers being so big that she couldn't swim in them, and other stupid comments." He shook his head in disgust. "My parents, on the other hand, did not try very hard to mask their relief. They must have feared I would really start dating Diana and they didn't like it. I imagine it was because of her father's position in the mill more than what they knew of her. I can only surmise this, but everyone talks so they might have gotten at least a little gossip about Diana's eccentricities. I'm sure they thought they were protecting their youngest son. They didn't want me tied up with a mill-worker's daughter." He looks at me.

"Even a farmer's daughter would be better than that, right?" I rarely say what goes through my mind and he looks shocked. What was I thinking to say something like that? I'm not interested in him. "Sorry. I guess it was a little of Diana seeping out. I didn't mean it that way."

"I know you probably don't think much of my family." Jacob is almost apologetic. "But I am not like them. I don't think of myself as one of the 'elite' in town."

He goes on. "I loved Diana because of her wildness and fearlessness, because she wasn't afraid to push the boundaries, to shock people, to explore new ideas. She wasn't like anyone I have ever known. I didn't care if she was poor. But they sure did." He nods in the direction of his house. I watch his sincere declaration. He loved her surely, but was it because she was different, because she wasn't afraid to be herself? Did he perhaps also want to trouble his parents, to rebel against them in the only way he knew how? He stares beyond me, seeing a vision of another time. Finally he says, "She made me laugh. She had as little regard for my brothers as they had for her. She said they were just younger cut-outs of my father." His eyes search mine. I think he is alluding to the rumor that his father is a philanderer and as a local town official got into trouble with the wife of another town official. The whole town buzzed about it. I look at him, nodding, trying to show by my expression that I've heard the rumor. No wonder he wants to rebel.

Jacob continues. "My mother is afraid of him. He can have a terrible temper. She tries to keep him happy, and if he lies to her she doesn't question him. She stays home most of the time because he doesn't like her to go out. He's probably afraid someone might say something to her. She accepts it. She doesn't have any backbone."

So, I think, here is another example of why Diana was a powerful draw for him. She, quirky as she was, did have a backbone. I feel sad for him.

"Sometimes," he says, "I feel like I don't even belong in my family. I feel as though the stork dropped me at the wrong chimney. Do you ever feel like that?"

"No. I love my family and I feel like I belong exactly where I've landed. Well, you know, we're not a perfect family. We bicker and disagree, but I think that's normal."

"So what do we do next?" It sounds like he wants to move on.

"I'll ask Grace to give me the name of that boy from Diana's biology class, and I'll try to find out more. At some point I'd like to get to talk to Jeffrey." He looks surprised, but nods his head. "Good idea. I'll try to ask around more too."

"Should we get some studying done while we're here?" Jacob nods yes and we both start reading our textbooks in earnest.

Chapter 6 – Jeffrey

I think we need to talk to the Turners to get an understanding of Diana's home life, in hopes of constructing a better picture. Every bit of information we collect will help us in our effort to unravel the hidden story.

I start by looking for Jeffrey on his way home. Several years ago, after graduating from high school, he began working at the mill while still living at home with his parents. He seems like a nice quiet boy. Like Diana he is a slim and neat package, with the same fine light brown hair, dark brows and pock-marked skin. He has sharp features and quick eyes. He looks intelligent even before he opens his mouth. Although I've seen him only in school as an upperclassman, I've heard he is as reserved as Diana and almost as eccentric. He likes to hunt and fish and spends a lot of time in the woods, and I've heard he even builds rough little hideaways there where he stays overnight for several days at a time.

I think if I walk on the path down by the river I might catch him taking the shortcut home between his house and the mill. When I get out of school I run home, do a couple of quick chores, and promise to be back later to finish up. I put on trousers and walk briskly down to where the path to the mill cuts in. The opening is wide and well-used by the villagers to get to the mill and also to fish. I know when the shifts let out and I am there early. I hear the sounds at the mill, the sawing, grinding and other mechanical noises. I pick up a branch and break off the smaller pieces to make myself a walking-staff, much like I'd seen Diana do a number of times. I wander along intersecting paths, trying to look like a casual stroller in the woods. I hear the whistle that signals the shift change, and turn back towards where I think

Jeffrey will be making his way, and as I do a voice calls from behind me, "Hanna? Is that you, Hanna? What are you doing out here?" I am startled when Jeffrey comes up behind me. Too surprised and embarrassed to be clever, I give him an honest answer. "Actually, I was waiting for you."

"Really?" Now *he* seems surprised.

"How are you, Jeffrey?" I open with a thoughtful question. He pauses and faces me. "I'm okay. I'm doing okay. Is that why you were looking for me? To ask me that?"

"No. Of course I am concerned about you and your parents, but that isn't why I am out here."

"Okay," he says as he turns back to the path, steps in front of me and starts up the hill.

"I want to know what happened, what led up to it."

"You know," Jeffrey replies, "my mother is angry with you and suspicious of you. She wonders why you weren't with Diana and what did happen."

"I understand. I don't know what happened. I don't know why she was out wandering around. We hadn't made any plans to meet; I just stopped over to see her. She had seemed upset when I saw her at church that morning, but I wasn't sure why, so I wanted to see her." From the back I can see Jeffrey nod.

"I know she did seem upset. She had been getting angrier and almost irrational the last few weeks before it happened. I asked her about it but she didn't seem to have an explanation. Sometimes it would be about the dog not behaving and running off, sometimes it would be about school, sometimes about that Sparks guy. She just wasn't herself."

"Yeah," I agree, "she had been angry. I thought it was someone at school that was bothering her. You know sometimes people enjoyed harassing her. Most of the time she liked to pretend it didn't bother her, and she didn't want to let on when it did."

Jeffrey stops short. "You know, there was someone in one of her classes who she said had been bothering her, but I thought he stopped."

"Yes, yes, Grace mentioned someone was teasing her or something. Do you remember his name?"

"No. He was a new student this year. He just moved into town. That's all I remember."

"I'll try to find out more about him, and I'll let you know if it seems important."

Jeffrey continues walking and talking. "I miss her." His voice seems to tremble and he slows a little, but he doesn't stop. "She was quirky and full of life, new ideas, always interesting, usually on an adventure. I think she got a lot of her ways from our mother. Mom was the nature-lover and the one always interested in new things. Dad didn't seem to give a hoot. He just wanted to be left alone. He'd sit for hours reading the paper and listening to the radio. He didn't want to try new things or go, as he said, 'traipsing through the GD woods.' He and Diana would have run-ins sometimes, especially when she was trying to take care of a new animal or protect one. He'd stomp on a mouse if it wasn't fast enough and take pride in it. He did it just to upset her. So if he found out she was sneaking food out of the house for one of her critters, he'd blow his stack." Jeffrey slows and turns slightly so I can see his silhouette. "Now? He wouldn't kill a spider. He says Diana wouldn't like it."

He turns back up the path and continues walking. "Well, I've got to get into the house or Ma will be worried. Here I am twenty years old and they worry more than ever."

I touch his arm slightly from behind. "Thanks for taking the time to talk to me. Can we talk again soon?" He looks back and nods. I say, "What about next week? I also have a favor to ask." Jeffrey stops again, turns and says, "Sure. What do you want?"

I hesitate. "Diana had a diary." I pause to see any signs that he knows about it. "Could I get a look at it? I wouldn't want to keep it. I just want to see it." I hope that my demeanor conveys my earnestness.

"Are you looking for clues?"

"Yes, I guess I am." I don't want to tell him I am working on this with 'that Sparks boy,' as he calls Jacob. It seems like he doesn't think much of him. "And maybe you shouldn't tell your mother."

He doesn't hesitate long. "Okay, let me see what I can do. We haven't done much with her room yet."

A thought occurs to me, "Well, maybe you could let me in, you know, let me look around her room? I'd be careful not to disturb anything. Is there a time when your mother is going out?"

He looks keenly at me, trying, I think, to see if I have other motivations. "Yeah, she's got to go into the village Tuesday morning, I think. She works at the Cunninghams' on Tuesday mornings. Can you get out of school around 10:30? I'll run up from the mill during my break. But you have to promise to be careful and not let anyone know, because if she hears third-hand we'll both be in deep…"

"Oh, thank you. I really appreciate this. Tuesday at 10:30. I won't forget." I grab his elbow, surprising us both by giving him a light kiss on the cheek, and run off on the path back to the village. He looks after me, touches his cheek, and then turns up the cut-off towards his house.

When I meet Jacob I tell him everything Jeffrey told me. He isn't surprised; most of this he has heard or uncovered himself. He's heard about the boy in class and found out his name and more about him. Billy and his parents just moved into town from Norwich. They have relocated so his father can get a job at the mill. Jacob heard that Billy was a wiseacre and was getting into trouble in several of his classes, not just Diana's. He also heard he was bothering other girls and was warned about it. Jacob says Diana had mentioned many of the things I told him about her mother and father, so that wasn't news. But was any of it cause enough to upset Diana? We don't think so, unless there are things she didn't tell us, or things no one is telling us.

Jacob is becoming more comfortable around me and I around him. We are getting to know each other and become friends. I like him. He is kind and without complexities. He obviously cared for Diana. This is becoming our little obsession, this quest to find the truth about why Diana ended up in a pool on the Natchaug River.

I don't mention the planned meeting between Jeffrey and me on Tuesday. I told Jeffrey I wouldn't tell anyone and I will keep my word.

Chapter 7 - The Diary

I do something on Tuesday that I very rarely do. I lie. I fake a stomachache to get out of my morning classes so I can escape to meet Jeffrey. The only problem will be to sneak through town without being seen by the villagers. Everyone knows kids should be in school weekday mornings, and everyone knows most of the kids in school including me. We walk through the village every day on our way to and from school. How can I get through town either without being seen or with a viable reason to be out of school? It would certainly get back to my parents. Should I feign my stomachache, rush to the Turners' and get the diary and then rush home so that it seems like I truly am sick? The distance from the edge of the village to the Turners' is not far and few people live in that area. I may be able to pull it off.

So at 10:15 I put on a pained expression, hold my stomach and raise my hand to ask to go to the bathroom. When I get back I ask to leave and am granted permission to go home. I grab my coat and books and head out the door and through the village as I would normally to go home, but at the turn-off to our farm I keep going. I walk briskly to the edge of the village and up the road towards the Turners'. When I arrive and find Jeffrey not yet there, I walk down the path a little way towards the mill, not wanting to be seen up near the road or loitering around their empty house. I think I hear someone in the house and when I look back it seems to me that the curtains flutter in the upstairs eaves bedroom that was Diana's. Startled, I steady myself against a tree and watch the window for more movement, but I see nothing. As I stand there watching the house I hear Jeffrey coming up the path. He's moving quickly, almost running.

"Hanna, hurry; we've got to move quickly. I've got to get back to the mill in a few minutes." He passes me and pulls me along by my arm. I trip, dust myself off and follow him. He is now a dozen strides in front of me and seems impatient with my clumsiness. Cecil, Diana's crow, caws madly at us. We get to the back door and he dashes in, rushing up the stairs and beckoning to me.

"Hurry. We have only a minute." He opens the door and shows me in. "I think the diary is over there." He points towards a table in the corner that Diana used as a desk. Nostalgia almost overcomes me. In the rush to get the diary I didn't think of the emotional toll this task would cost me. I look around the room and the memories flood back. Wasn't it only three weeks ago that Diana and I sat here plotting one scheme or another? How we would pass our history test or how to get Jacob to hold her hand or what it must be like to kiss a boy. I try to suppress the tears that well up. Jeffrey is impatient. "Over there." He points again. I go to the table and pick up the diary. Her pen is there and I take that too, along with her precious quartz crystal that she used to rub for luck.

"Do you think I could have these too?" He nods impatiently. Then I see the Raggedy Anne doll on the bed and go over to look at it.

Jeffrey rushes over behind me, grabs my arm and pulls me around to face him. Without hesitating he pulls me close and roughly tries to kiss me.

I am defenseless, my arms pinned against my sides. The diary and pen drop to the floor as I try to raise my hands to push him away. I turn my head to avoid him and he kisses the side of my face, then my neck. I continue to struggle and am finally able to push him away.

"I thought you wanted me." He looks at me with surprise and desperation. I must have a look of horror on my face, and I watch his expression change as he sees how shocked and frightened I am. His demeanor shifts from desire to anger and he growls menacingly, "Don't you dare tell anyone about this."

I bend down to grab the diary and the pen and rush out as he stands by the door. "Get home, little girl," he tosses after me as he follows me down the stairs. I hear him go into the bathroom as I tear out the door and along the road to my house.

I am almost running by the time I get home. No one is in the house. I rush up the stairs and into my room breathless and shaking. As I put the diary and pen under my pillow I start to sob. All the difficulties of the last few weeks flood out in my uncontrollable tears. I hear my mother come in and I try to stifle my sobs.

"Who's up there? Hanna, is that you?"

"Yes, Mom, I wasn't feeling good and they let me come home from school." I'm sure I don't look very good at this point, red-faced and still sweating from running home.

My mother comes up the stairs and into the room I share with two sisters.

"What's wrong?" She walks over to me looking concerned and puts her hand on my forehead.

"My stomach. I have a really bad stomachache."

"What did you eat? Do you think it's something you ate? Do you know if anyone else is sick?" I just raise my shoulders.

"Get into bed. I'll bring you up some tea." She goes downstairs and I undress, get into my nightgown and then start to shiver. I am still trembling when she comes in with a steaming pot of tea.

"I'm worried about you," she says as she again feels my forehead. "If you don't feel better in an hour I'm going to call the doctor. You look terrible." I nod and snuggle deeper into the covers as she pours the tea.

"Drink some of this if you can. It's peppermint; it should help your stomach." I reach out, trying not to spill any on the bed. I feel terrible. I have lied and skipped school, I've sneaked down to a dead friend's house and been attacked by her creepy brother and then come home to lie about it again. I want nothing more than to tell my mother what happened, but I cannot bring myself to. She would be so disappointed in me. This is not who I am, and yet here I am continuing to be dishonest. I am ashamed and think to myself that this is a life-changing moment, the moment when I am sealing the direction my life will take, when I no longer trust my parents to guide my moral compass. I feel confused and exhausted and soon fall into a fitful sleep.

I awake startled by the sounds of supper being served in the kitchen below. The mist of the dream of being submerged in water ebbs as I am torn between my family's supper and trying to regain that wisp of dream. The dream loses to my desire to join them downstairs. I reach under my pillow. That wasn't a dream; the diary is still there. All the events of the morning rush back to me. I need time to understand what happened, to make sense of those crazy hours, but I cannot do that now without forgoing supper, and I'm hungry, smelling the aroma of bread and roasted chicken wafting from below. I hear someone come slowly up the stairs. My sister Grace pokes her head in. "Are you awake?" I nod my head and in the dim light I can see she's carrying a tray.

"Ma thought you should eat if you can. I brought you some dinner…"

"Thanks." I try to sound sick. She brings it over and puts it on the table near the window.

"I hope you feel better," she says as she turns and goes back downstairs.

I am grateful for the food and go to sit where we sometimes do our homework, starting my supper away from my family. My mind goes over the day as I eat and then, without finishing, climb back into bed, turn on my bedside table light and pull out the diary.

I thumb quickly through it. There are not too many entries; the book is only a quarter full. I decide to start from the beginning. Her handwriting is odd, sometimes leaning to the right, sometimes to the left, and occasionally not tilted at all. Although the penmanship is not the best, it is generally not too difficult to read. The first entry is dated about a year ago. I'm hoping to find clues that make the nastiness of my day worth the difficulties.

Chapter 8 – First Entry, July 5, 1935

Diana Turner –
July 5ᵗʰ, 1935

I hate this town. People are so ignorant and small and without any original thinking or creativity. My classmates, all products of their narrow cookie-cutter imprint by conformist parents, hate me too. I don't care. I have a couple of good friends who don't think I'm evil or insane or unnatural. To them I am—well, I guess they think I'm quirky. The rest of these cretins can all go to hell if there is such a place.

The Haves, of which I am not one, don't even deign to look at me. The Have-Nots, of which I am one, look down upon me as though I were from another planet or sub-species. When will I be able to escape from this village of boredom and mediocrity? I ignore the vindictive and hateful people who try to make my existence a trial, since letting them know they might bother me would only give them a twisted satisfaction. Sick, they are all sick.

Of all my teachers, only my biology teacher, Mr. Anders, thinks I am smart, maybe even brilliant he says. The rest of them give me barely passing grades, but I don't care for their simplistic ideas any more than they try to understand mine. What can they do? Fail me? Who cares about their grading systems that are structured to benefit the boring boys of privilege?

I am fortunate to have a mother who understands and encourages me. I love her. She's smart and compassionate but unfortunately stuck in the life of a drudge. Why did she marry my father? I often ask myself that question. But occasionally I see a spark between them and I know it was something neither of them could control. It is a sad fate that economics left our little family on a budget that barely keeps us in food and clothing. Even before my father's accident (which I don't remember), we were not well enough off to afford simple luxuries that most families enjoy. My father did splurge one year and purchase a radio that he said was for all of us, and we do enjoy it, but he enjoys it the most and sits by it in the semi-darkness of the evening living room. Smoking and coughing, he seems barely part of the family. My mother is the heart and life of us. She has imparted her love of the forest, the river and the animals to me. She has given me the gift of curiosity. My father's only wish is that I marry someone who can provide for me, and hopefully soon. That is one of his few jokes... hopefully soon.

But why would I want marriage now? I am too young and have too much to see and do. I am the princess, the adventuress, the healer, the priestess born of the lowly parents. What a cruel accident of birth. Really though, when I think about it, if I had been born to wealth and comfort I would never have turned out to be the girl, the woman, I am today. I would likely have become lazy or pressed to be a lady and follow that careful social structure that churns out those little china dolls that I despise so much. Give me my trousers and walking stick and let me roam or curl up with my dog and a well-worn novel. I will not follow convention. I will not be saddled and broken. I will not be a silly mindless giggler. I am a woman of power destined to become a queen.

Oh, (sigh) who am I kidding? I will be someone's wife like all the other girls. I can only hope I can find a good man who will be interesting and decent and love me, as I have so much love to share. But who? When I watch the boys in my class they seem so young and immature, and none seem at all interested in me either. They want only the pretty girls with the smart clothes and stylish shoes. The most they want of me is to ask if I think so-and-so is interested in them or if she would like this-or-that. I am just the boys' sounding board for their aspiring romantic selections. I hate them all too. If they could only see me for who I am, how beautiful I am inside and how interesting. Mom says to 'forget about them' that they are too young and dull to be worth my time. She thinks some upperclassman who is not such a child will be interested in me, and not to worry yet, I'm still a girl. A girl, she says, but I am developing the appetites of a woman. When will someone see that?

Chapter 9 - Hanna

Diana is right, I decide as I close the diary and stuff it back under my pillow. This town has lots of ignorant and intolerant people. But not all of them.

I hear shuffling below and know my sisters will be up soon to do homework and get ready for another day. Grace arrives first. She opens her book and spreads out some lined paper.

"How are you feeling? I see it didn't affect your appetite much." Grace has a bit of a tone to her comment.

"I am feeling better. I'll bring that tray down. Thank you for bringing it up."

When Ida, her twin, arrives, Grace is already concentrating on the book and writing. Ida urges her to move her papers to give her more room and Grace complies. Once settled they work diligently. Under the ring of the lamplight, despite their youth they look the picture of two old spinsters. Oh, I think, if they could only see themselves they would be mortified.

I pick up the tray and go downstairs. The supper dishes have been washed and put away. My father is reading the paper in the living room while my mother darns socks under the same lamp he is using. My younger brothers and sister are finishing the outside chores, throwing a bit of hay to the cows and closing up the chickens in the coop. My mother looks up. "Are you feeling better? You look better than you did. Come here. Let me feel your forehead." I comply and she nods with satisfaction. "Do you think you'll be okay to go to school tomorrow?"

"Yes. I am feeling better." As I bring my tray to the kitchen and wash and put away my dishes I reflect on my simple life. I am so fortunate to have such a good family, loving parents, all the food I need. From the kitchen window I watch as the kerosene lantern goes from the chicken coop to the barn. I have siblings who are fairly kind to one another and I don't have to deal with all the strain that Diana seemed to have been under. I get good grades in school, and my teachers and classmates like me. I don't feel that the town hates me. Does this make me fortunate? Was Diana under the curse of her artistic nature, or were the townsfolk indeed as hateful as she suspected? What a burden to be bright and gifted but poor and misunderstood.

Suddenly the horror of my morning comes snapping back into my consciousness like a bolt of lightning. How could I have forgotten that already? I have to steady myself on the sink. What a horrible experience! What happened? What did I do? Was I stupid to go into that house with him? I had no idea he was going to attack me, no idea. He did not ever seem like someone who would do that. He seemed so caring, so nice. He seemed to really miss his sister a lot. I am lucky, I see now as I reflect. He could have hurt me, could have...

I am embarrassed that I was so gullible, so trusting. I don't feel as though I can tell my parents. For so many reasons I must keep this to myself, but I want to tell someone. My parents, always cautious, always telling us to be safe, and I walk right into a trap that I never saw. Did he plan this right from the beginning, or was it something hatched at that moment? I actually liked him and perhaps had a small crush on him. The times that I saw him when I visited Diana's he was so nice. Now I have only horrible thoughts and fears. I cannot believe this has happened to me.

I see the lantern moving again from the barn, coming towards the house.

My sister and brothers come in, clapping their hands and blowing out the lantern. "Geeze, it's cold out there. Can we throw a couple extra logs on tonight?" I hear my father's paper rustle. "Sure, but not big ones. I don't want to be up all night waiting for them to burn down." He's speaking loud enough for them to hear him in the kitchen. Cyrus goes to the wood box on the porch and brings in a small armload of oak. He opens the stove door and pushes the pieces in one at a time. My sister asks me how I'm feeling. I say I'm okay and we all exchange small talk: one of the cows needs more hay than usual, the chickens are still laying pretty well, a mouse startled in the grain bin jumped out and up my brother's arm and Amy laughed when he screamed.

We all start towards our rooms, our parents saying goodnight as we climb the stairs.

Ida is still working as I go in but Grace seems about to finish. "Hanna? Jacob was looking for you today when school let out. He wanted to know where you were. What's going on with you two?"

"Oh, nothing. We've just gotten together a few times to talk about Diana. He misses her." I try to moderate my tone, sounding casual. I'm worried that people will notice our collaboration and think there is something going on between Jacob and me. I know I shouldn't feel guilty. We are, after all, meeting about Diana and there is nothing going on.

"Well, if you're going to school tomorrow, and you look well enough to me to be able to go, be sure to speak to him. He seemed concerned."

Jacob. How can I tell him what I did? I can't, but how can I not? Should I tell him about the diary? He'll ask about finding it. I just cannot talk to him about it yet.

I think about Diana's words, about how she felt so many were against her. Were they? I know that people thought her weird and maybe even troubled. My parents at times even questioned my judgment, but when she visited she was polite to them and they could see she wasn't a bad girl.

The librarian liked her. Diana visited the library often and took out as many books as were allowed, and when she returned them she liked to talk to the librarian about them. The librarian thought she was very bright and enjoyed having such a lively inquisitive girl visit so often.

The shopkeeper did not seem to like her. If Diana went in he would watch her as though he expected her to steal something. She wasn't a thief. She was only poor.

I know that Jacob's parents didn't like her, but their fears were groundless. She was not scheming to marry into their family. She was interested in Jacob not because he was more well-to-do but because he was kind to her.

Mr. Anders? I know she liked him. I've heard odd things about him, that he sometimes accompanies students home when they have to stay late after school, that he mentors and tutors students more than the other teachers do. I've heard he was strict but also that he had favorites. I think that is nothing. Kids talk, but nothing really definite is said. Probably it was just kids wanting to get back at someone who reprimanded them. When Diana heard them talk about him she would defend him.

From the sound of her diary there were others who didn't like her, but what of that? Would that be a motive to hurt her, or was it just that they made her so sad she didn't want to face them anymore? I doubt that she was someone who gave up or gave in. She was a fighter.

My mind goes through the village, one house after another. Who in this house wouldn't like her and why? Who in that house? I am drowsy and fall asleep envisioning this virtual village walk.

I am floating, relaxed and drifting, but when I take a breath I choke. I'm breathing water. I sit upright, awake, gasping. My chest is heaving and I try to catch my breath to slow my pounding heart. I am in my bed. I'm in my home with my family.

I am okay. I am not drowning. I lie back down. A flash of remembrance grips me, but flashes as quickly away. I pray for sleep. I don't want to remember.

Chapter 10 – The Sparkses

Jacob and I have met several times at the library. The librarian likely accepts this as a natural outcome of two people who have united in grief over the loss of their mutual friend. She sees us studying and talking and, knowing both our families, probably assumes we might make a good match someday. Several classmates have seen us working together, and a little gossip has gotten back to us about it. We feel totally innocent in this alliance, although we've heard that some are speculating that there is more to this than just meeting for homework and conversation about our friend.

So far my family has not heard the gossip or I would certainly have gotten comments from Grace. Jacob's family, however, has noticed, and his brothers have spoken to him, making jokes. When he tries to explain he blushes and becomes too tongue-tied to finish. He is so sweet and innocent. His brothers are probably just trying to toughen him up. I like him, and can understand how Diana found herself drawn to him. He is honest and without guile. His dark curly hair is bent over his book, trying to concentrate. I want to pat him like a puppy. I'm sure he would not have approached me without the excuse of our shared friendship. He's too shy for that, but, like Diana, once a bond has been established and the shyness buffed away, the interesting and thoughtful person shines through.

He's not a scholar and must study hard to get decent grades, unlike his brothers, who seemed able to breeze through secondary school without effort. He's a good-looking young man who will probably grow into a handsome man like his father, although with luck he may not inherit his father's values. I've overheard my parents calling Mr. Sparks a small-town scoundrel.

When you see his mother she gives you the impression of a proud and refined woman, but I've heard that her husband is cruel to her and she dares not cross him or he will publicly humiliate her. Jacob adores his mother and that is another source of friction with his brothers, who have learned their father's disdain for her. It is interesting that the well-to-do don't always have the life of ease we would expect. When I see Mrs. Sparks at the market or in church she acknowledges me with a nod, which Diana said was more than she would get.

Jacob told Diana that his father had taken to humiliating him too. Diana said that Jacob is strong-willed and does not bend under his father's pressure, which instead seems to bind him closer to his mother. Sometimes, Diana said, his mother tries to push him away, hoping to deflect some of the ire that rains upon both of them. Jacob neither respects nor fears his father. Diana thought Jacob knew a secret that protected him, but he never said that directly.

All the effort that Jacob's parents put into diverting his interest in Diana produced little actual movement away from her. Jacob found in Diana a person who was honest, direct and trustworthy. She was also enough of a rebel to be intriguing to a boy from an outwardly staid and seemingly conservative family. His father tossed off sordid comments about his dating "poor white trash," hoping to bring his son to his senses somehow. His brothers had almost given up on him and told him he'd never get anywhere in life with a woman like that. If he wanted to succeed, they said, he'd need someone who came from a good family with better breeding. Jacob thought this was silly, as though their family was anything but small-town aristocracy, if that. His mother secretly sided with Jacob, but kept silent when the others were riding him. She once said that all of their railing would only send Jacob into Diana's arms. That comment made them pause, but they had so little respect for her opinion that they were soon throwing jabs at him again.

They commented on Diana's plain dresses and worn-down shoes, and her tromping through the woods in trousers. They talked about the prettier and more prominent girls in school with fancy dresses and nice shoes who came from good families. Why didn't he like them? He sometimes wondered about that himself, but quickly realized those girls were silly and shallow, and gossiped and made hateful comments about other people. He told himself it wasn't that he wanted to shame his family or somehow retaliate for their snobbery. He really did like Diana. It was that simple.

Gilbert Sparks, Senior was obsessed with the affair between Jacob and Diana. He called it an affair because he could never imagine having a woman as a friend. Women were for two things, and one of them was keeping the house. He could not understand why his son would have a girlfriend and not be bedding her. Even the idea that it would be possible sent him into fits of rage that he aimed at his wife, ranting that she turned him into a sissy boy—why else wouldn't he be just having this little tramp and be done with her?

He heard of Jacob's meetings with me from his son Gilbert junior, who seemed to be privy to more gossip than anyone else. When did he have time to spy, since he was supposed to be studying at the local college? Gilbert senior was troubled by this. Was it another sexless liaison with a classmate? What were we doing together? All this I got from Jacob, who describes angry harangues from his father. Jacob is close to stopping our trysts at the library when we launch a plan to involve Fannie. We will meet a little earlier, discuss what we have found, perhaps even exchange notes which would take less time, and then Fannie will meet us and we'll all study together. We hope this will lessen the tension in the Sparks household.

On the way home from our second meeting with Fannie, we part as I start up the road toward my house. In the dusk I can see on the corner a figure I do not recognize. I have never felt afraid in town—I know most of the villagers and the neighbors are almost like family—but the figure does not seem familiar. For the first time in my life I am frightened, but I do not waver. I turn the corner towards our farm and the person calls my name. I pause.

"Hanna? What are you doing with my brother? Are you two trying to be detectives? What do you think you'll find? If you're smart, and I think you are, you'll stay away from him. You just never know what kind of creatures haunt these woods looking for schoolgirls." Gilbert Sparks says these last words with an oddly evil-sounding sneer. I don't say a word, but walk briskly to my house. The warm light pouring from the windows embraces me. I am home and I have more to think about.

Chapter 11 – Second Entry - Friends

Why would Gilbert threaten me? Jacob says his family frequently harasses him over his personal life. They want total control over whom he sees, why he sees them and what he does with them. But why would they threaten me? What do I do now? Do I tell Jacob about this? Do I tell him we have to stop? Or do we press on, being more secretive?

I decide to write him a note, telling him what happened and suggesting we do our searching separately and write our findings in letters, exchanging them once a week.

I try to sleep but cannot, so again I open Diana's diary.

Diana Turner
October 15th, 1935

Jacob Sparks has been following us home from school. At first I thought he was just weird. Then I thought he was interested in Fannie or Hanna, but now as they reach their homes he continues on with me. WITH ME! I think he likes me. It is unbelievable. Finally the poor millworker's daughter will be the princess. He is quite handsome. He is young, and has acne, but that is of no mind to me. He is not a bragger boy like so many, showing off or teasing. He is earnest and kind. He's not overwhelmingly bright, but he's not a dullard either. I've talked to Hanna about him and she agrees that he is a good man and likes me and is not out to take advantage of me. He is not at all like his brothers. Gilbert, his oldest brother, once pushed me around the side of the school building and started kissing me with these messy, slobbering kisses. I was disgusted and screamed and he let me go, saying as I rushed away that most girls would give their right eye to make out with him. What a creep. No, he is nothing like his brother. His other brother is nicer but they are both cut from the same cloth as their father. Only Jacob favors his mother. It is no matter really, as his parents don't seem to like me. I will always be the poor millworker's daughter. In my dreams I rise above my station, but the reality is that it is impossible. Still, Jacob likes me and that is enough for now.

Of all the people who come near our house, only Hanna and Jacob are safe from the cawing wrath of Cecil. Cecil knows good people, and warns me of the bad. So does Harry, Harry my faithful wolfhound. When life sometimes seems bleak, my friends, two- and four-footed, carry me through.

It was a warm and sunny day and now closing towards evening. The dusk, almost here, is my favorite time of day, when the world pauses and sighs before the night brings rest. At least rest for some, but wandering and scavenging for others. Some days seem right. The river's distant yet incessant roar is always in my ears. Only if I walk upriver far enough can I hear the gentle murmur of the smaller pools or the quiet of the deeper forest. I'm off now to take Harry for a walk before it gets dark. Some days it all seems right.

Chapter 12 – A Thief

I have vowed not to give up searching for clues. I don't see Diana as a person so desperate as to kill herself. The plan that Jacob and I have of working together to find out what happened is still in place. However, we must be more furtive or it may cause us more trouble. We hope to continue separately and only now and then will we meet, secretly, to exchange what we have found. We listen and watch and wait. People who know we are friends of Diana's come up to us with little tales of their interactions with her, and this is proving to be a great help to us.

One person told Jacob that he thought Diana was unpredictable like a wild animal and seemed to be getting wilder all the time. Jacob asked him what he meant and he said she was always wandering in the woods and could disappear and appear like a wraith. He said he often saw her upriver from the pools, and in the summer he said he sometimes saw her sunbathing there. Jacob let him talk and he bragged about seeing her swimming nude in the pools and once she saw him and told her dog to go after him. The dog chased him until finally from a long distance he could hear Diana's whistle, at which the dog stopped short and turned back. He said he was never so frightened in his life. Jacob heard a couple of similar stories from other acquaintances. He was surprised he'd never heard such things before, and thought it unlikely that all these boys had the same experience. He thought perhaps it had happened to one and the others were just repeating it. He thought they were mostly fabrication and he was not ascribing them much significance.

A couple of people told me they thought she was crazy, or a witch. None of this was new. I'd heard it before and also did not pay it much heed.

I decide to find out more if I can, in what might be the best place. I know Mrs. Turner works in the village on Tuesdays. During school vacation this week I will try to get into Diana's room once again, this time without Jeffrey's help.

I wait in the village until I see Mrs. Turner pass through town. She has a bundle with her, which I surmise is a bunch of rags. When she is out of sight I walk briskly toward the Turner house. If possible I don't want anyone in the village to see me. Once I get close, I begin to lose my nerve. What was I thinking? But having gotten this far and knowing that I will not likely get this opportunity again, I walk around to the back door that Jeffrey let me through over a month ago. I am grateful no snow has yet fallen; I would certainly have left telltale footprints. As I reach the door and put my hand on the handle I hear a loud shriek that buckles my knees and almost throws me to the ground. Again the shriek: "Cheeee!" At that moment I realize it is Cecil. He has landed just above me in a low-hanging branch and is calling to me, just as he would Diana.

"Oh Cecil, you frightened the death out of me." I make a familiar whistle I'd heard Diana make to him and he flies even closer, lands on the ground by me, prances around and looks at me sideways. "Are you missing Diana? I bet you're hungry. Let me see if I can find a crumb for you." As I go in Cecil flies back up into the tree and watches the door with a steady gaze, rocking side to side on the branch.

I step through the threshold and am almost knocked over again. It is Harry this time. Gigantic paws on my shoulders, he laps my face like a long-lost lover. Oh dear, these poor animals. Who is giving them the love they once had lavished on them so generously? I pat Harry and talk to him as I walk through the house and up the stairs to Diana's bedroom. "Harry, how have you been? I bet you miss Diana, don't you? Will you help me find a clue? Do you know what happened?" I go on and on like this in a low voice trying to calm Harry and myself. The door to her bedroom is closed. "Harry, you'll have to wait out here, okay? But I'll tell you what I find." I shut the door behind me on a whimpering Harry. "Okay, Harry, I hear you. I'll be back out in a second." All this and lots more I say while my eyes adjust to the darkened room and I try to scan for something that might tell me more.

The pen and quartz crystal are back on the table where I found them that day I came up here with Jeffrey. I shudder to think about that and what might have happened. The bed has been straightened and everything looks as it did. I walk over to look at the Raggedy Ann I didn't get to see that day. Picking her up I find a crushed handkerchief stuffed under the pillow beneath her. It is stained and crusty with something dried. Disgusted, I try to push the thing back under the pillow while touching it as little as possible. I don't even want to think about what it might be. Was Jeffrey molesting his sister? Is this the secret clue we're looking for? I store this away in my mind and move around the room in the semi-darkness. On her dresser is a small comb-and-brush set. On the table by the window lie a couple of school books and papers and her change purse. I part the curtain enough to shed a little more light on the table. I open her biology book and find graded tests and homework with Mr. Anders's notes on them. "A+. Great job. You have a future in biology!" "A-. See me after class on this one. I think your ideas are exciting." Thumbing through the papers I find a folded one, a note. I unfold it and read, "Tell him he had better leave you alone or I will KILL HIM!" There is no signature, no clue to the writer or the target of the threat.

This is shocking! I fold up the note along with a couple of the biology tests and papers. I look through some of the other books but find nothing. Her piles of books about music, art, religion, science, graphology, animals and alchemy are in a corner with some candles, Tarot cards and a small dagger. Where did she get that and what did she use it for? I'm beginning to feel like I didn't know her as well as I thought. I want to take the Raggedy Ann but know it would be missed. I stuff into my bag the items I thought special to her: pen, Tarot cards, dagger, quartz crystal, and the book on handwriting analysis, into which I tuck the folded papers. I hook the bag over my shoulder and go out to the whimpering Harry. He greets me again as though I've been gone for months.

In the kitchen I find some bread and I give Harry a slice and take another out to Cecil. Cecil caws at me, flies to the ground and pulls at the slice I throw down to him, standing on it with one foot and pecking it apart. He eyes me as I leave but is too busy with the bread to be bothered to follow or call out. As I slide along the side of the house out of view of the village my fear grows again. What if someone sees me? After surveying the road and finding it empty, I quickly step out onto it and walk along briskly, trying to be nonchalant. I am not caught. I'm excited but heave a big sigh of relief. I DID IT! I am a thief!

Chapter 13 – Not Guilty

I cannot wait to see Jacob. I feel like a real detective. Is this what they do, real detectives? Do they use nefarious means to find clues, to find the guilty party? I won't get to see him until school starts next week. I don't dare try to meet with him before then.

After finishing all my chores and the homework assigned us for vacation, I ponder what else I can do to find clues. I volunteer to go to the market for my mother and there I spend time at the counter talking to neighbors. Most of them are very kind and remember that Diana and I were friends and tell me they are sorry about her. They ask about her family, but I have nothing to tell them. Now I feel ashamed for turning away from Diana's family, who once welcomed me. I have gone into their house and taken some of Diana's possessions. I am a thief and a disloyal friend. I should go talk to her mother, explain to her that I don't know what happened and ask her why she is blaming me. I don't know for certain that she is blaming me; I only remember her pointing that finger at me during the funeral. I can still see that and it gives me the chills.

On Sunday after church my mother takes me aside. "People have been talking and it has gotten back to me."

"What do you mean?" I don't understand what she's talking about.

"Hanna, how can you act like you don't know?" I shrug my shoulders, still not understanding. "They say something is going on with you and Jacob. Do you know what I mean now?"

"There's nothing going on between me and Jacob. We're just friends. What have you heard?"

"The librarian thinks you're plotting something, or that you *did* plot something. You both knew Diana and maybe you wanted to see each other..." I am shocked and my face must be showing it. "What? I cannot believe this! Just because we study together sometimes?"

"And," my mother continues, "some people at the market think you're suspiciously spying around, fishing for information as though you were guilty."

"Some people at the market?" My tone rises. "This is insane! What are they thinking? I hardly even knew Jacob before Diana died. We hardly ever talked before then."

"And—" she pauses for full effect—"Jacob's parents apparently think you're no better an influence on Jacob than Diana was. They spoke to me themselves and said they told Jacob to stay away from you."

"Oh my goodness, this *is* crazy!" I am truly shocked. I sit on the bed with a thousand thoughts racing through my head. Minutes ago I was trying to find out what happened and now I am the accused. Suddenly I realize this is probably a diversion. This is a diversion by the guilty party to deflect attention from himself. That must be it. How else could anyone think this way? "So, what do *you* think?"

"Of course I think this is silly. If Jacob is anything like the rest of his family you wouldn't have anything to do with him. I trust your judgment that much. But it doesn't matter what I think. When people talk it's the talk that's dangerous. It doesn't have to be real. It sticks in their stupid heads anyway and they will always think of it when they see you. After a while it's hard to determine what is rumor and what is truth."

"Jacob is not like his family." I wanted to set that record straight. "He's kind and thoughtful and sincere..." I stop, realizing I may have revealed a bit too much, not just to my

70

mother but maybe to myself also. "Anyway, he's not like his family."

"How do you know? Do you really know him? How long have you been studying together? If there is something wrong, if someone has done something wrong, I don't want you to be implicated. Right now, spending time with him may be putting you in bad company. Innocent or not, let's not give people a chance to talk more."

I look straight at her. I'm angry, hurt and surprised. "I can't believe you're telling me to avoid him. That's what you're telling me, right? You've never done this before. Don't you trust me?"

"Darling Hanna, I would never do anything to hurt you. I am only looking out for your best interest."

"But you're treating me like a child who cannot think for herself, who cannot negotiate the tricky current of adulthood."

"You are still young. You may be smart, but you haven't had enough experience to understand what gossip can do to your reputation. I've seen people ruined over nothing, over a misunderstanding. Please trust me on this. I won't tell your Papa. Let's just keep this between us."

"Okay," I say sulkily, but I know I have to keep seeing Jacob, even if just once more to tell him what I've found. It all depresses me. I am allowing myself to be dragged deeper and deeper into dishonesty. Is this worth it? Will it be worth it? What if we find nothing? She's gone; does it matter anymore? And what of Jacob? Is he really as he seems to me or is it just a charade, just an act to ensnare me as he did Diana?

As my mother descends the stairs she calls over her shoulder, "Come on down and help us cook dinner."

"Be right there."

My mind goes over the things I found at Diana's. The pen is in my purse with the cards. The quartz and dagger are under my pillow along with the papers that I tucked into an envelope. I have gone through the papers carefully, reading through the lessons and homework and tests that were my friend's work. Looking at her handwriting and clever answers to questions I could not have answered, I was again amazed by her intelligence. She remembered terms with such clarity. Seeing all this made me sad. Mr. Anders was impressed; he said she had so much promise, that she had an original mind. Was there more to it? Was she really that smart or was he trying to manipulate her, trying to reach that more vulnerable spot by flattering her? She was certainly good at biology, but was she *that* good? What did they talk about when they got together after class? Was it always about the class or were there more personal discussions? Maybe she talked about how she felt like an outcast and maybe he understood and tried to tell her how little other people's opinions mattered. All this is conjecture; I don't know anything for sure. I only know that he liked her and thought she was smart and that she liked him and he made her feel special.

The bigger puzzle piece is exciting and frightening. Who wrote that threatening note and why? It was written on white unlined paper. No clues there. It looks like it was written with a pencil. No clues there. The handwriting is longhand, not halting like a young person's writing, not flowing with the smoothness of an elegant hand. I have taken the time to compare the handwriting of Mr. Anders and the mystery note. They don't look totally similar although there are a few common characteristics. I've decided it is unlikely that Mr. Anders wrote it. I make a copy with carbon paper, tracing it with a dry pen, and thumb through the book on handwriting analysis. I believe I must try to get samples of other people's handwriting to compare to this. How can I do that? And who should be first?

Chapter 14 – Third Entry – Innocent?

Back at school after vacation I pass Jacob a note after our first class:

> *I have been forbidden to see you.*
> *We must be secretive.*
> *I have information to share with you.*
> *Can we meet after dinner tonight, 8 p.m.?*
> *On the corner? I'll be there. I hope you will.*

I hope he will be able to meet me. I am so excited about all the information I've uncovered. I don't know how to tell him that I found the diary. I don't know how to tell him I've broken into the Turners' home and stolen Diana's private property. I don't know how to tell him Jeffrey is dangerous and may be a suspect. I don't know how to ask him for a sample of his brother's and his father's handwriting, realizing as I say this that I think they too are implicated.

The school day goes by painfully slowly. I don't care about my schoolwork. I only want to gather information and to see if Jacob has found anything.

Finally school lets out and I nonchalantly walk home with friends, heading up to the farm to do my chores, eat supper, finish the little homework I have left and then walk to the corner to meet Jacob. When I see a clock it seems that time is moving impossibly slowly. Finally, at a few minutes to eight, I dress warmly and tell anyone listening that I'm going for a walk and I'll be back in a few minutes. No one seems to be paying any attention so I leave and walk briskly towards the corner.

It is dark and very chilly. We don't have snow yet but it is beginning to feel like we will soon. Most puddles are frozen and I can see my breath when I exhale a large lungful of air. I didn't bring a flashlight but a waxing moon gives me enough light to see the road, and even makes faint shadows of the bare trees across the way. I get to the corner a minute or so before eight. As I wait under the oak, sounds of the cold wintry evening interrupt the quiet. An owl's "hoot-hoot, hoot-hoooo" is quickly followed by scurrying in the leaves. A more distant snapping of twigs announces a deer trying to pick its way quietly through the woods. As I listen there is more scurrying here and snapping there, then the owl hoots again and dogs bark. A screech makes me jump— is it an owl or a fisher cat or a bobcat? Even though I doubt anything will attack me the sounds are chilling. I am starting to be concerned about Jacob. I think I've been here fifteen minutes and still he isn't coming. Perhaps I should not have given him that time. Maybe it wasn't convenient and he had no way of telling me. I decide to wait a few more minutes. One of the cats that followed me from the farm is pushing itself against my legs. "Well, Ralph, I guess he's not coming." As I speak there is a startled rustling in the leaves nearby, but no one comes down the road. "Let's go back, Ralph," I say as I turn around. Bending to pet the cat, I head disappointedly back to the farm.

As I get into bed my mind goes over the possibilities. What happened to Jacob? Sleeplessness and thoughts about our next steps drive me to the diary again.

Diana Turner
January 12th, 1936

It is freezing in the house, bone-chilling. I am writing with a blanket over my lap and another over my shoulders. My father scrimps on coal and many of the radiators emanate nothing but cold. Only once in a while with loud clanging does the steam come on and hiss for a few minutes before it stops again. When I was young he would send me out with my wagon to pick up coal that had fallen from the train. At that age I thought it fun, but I don't want to do it now.

I am grateful for Harry, who lies full-length next to me in bed and keeps one side of me warm. But I worry for Cecil sitting on the branch outside looking longingly into the house. I wonder what my parents would do if I opened the window and let him in. I wonder if he would be quiet and in the morning fly out without a fuss. At least I was able to give him some table scraps that Harry wouldn't eat. That should help him keep warm tonight.

When I get into bed and try to get warm, I imagine that instead of the big wolfhound beside me I have a handsome fellow. I dream of Jacob and hug Harry, who licks my face sloppily. Jacob. He still walks with me and we often walk in the woods together and talk of our home life and our dreams. His father is very hard on him and constantly compares him to his brothers. Jacob says he doesn't ever want to be like his brothers and he just hopes he can hold on long enough to get into college and away from the negative atmosphere. He worries though that his father will not fund his college tuition if he doesn't follow the rules. First he must get good grades. He struggles to do so and studies much more than most people I know. Then his father wants him to adhere to the values he holds dear, ones which place money and power ahead of people with little concern for honesty in business dealings or personal life. Jacob says he knows his father cheats on his mother and it doesn't seem to bother his conscience whatsoever. His father wants him to be more like his brothers, who are without concern for consequences to others, thinking only of themselves.

Only once did I see in him a flash of the Sparks value system (as he calls his father's attitude). One day when Harry came rushing up Jacob kicked him away, asking why I would cherish such a dirty dog. Of course Harry loves everyone and wants to lick them all and get his ears scratched and head patted. Good-natured Harry ignored the kick and was still friendly to Jacob. Harry knew I liked Jacob so he accepted him. I explained to Jacob how important Harry was to me, how much he filled that sometimes empty place. He was my always accepting and loving friend, always happy to see me, always willing to go for a walk, always wanting to spend time with me. How could I not value such a wonderful animal? Jacob's attitude switched quickly, but I had seen his flash of intolerance.

Jacob? After reading this entry in the diary I start to think about him. Is he really as good and kind as I think? Or is he working with me because he can manipulate my search and findings? Can he be protecting his family, or even in an indirect way be guilty himself? Where was he tonight? Was his family keeping him from going out or did he himself not want to see me? Have I come to a dead-end in my search? My mother is against it, and who else?

I hope I can get to sleep. I start to drift off and awake with a start, choking. I can't get my breath. Is this what it is like to drown?

Chapter 15 - Caught

At school I am surprised to find that Jacob is absent today. I heard a classmate say he is sick. When they call his name in class and he doesn't answer, several heads turn to look at me. I fix my gaze on the teacher, pretending not to see the stares. She goes on to the next name.

I wonder why he is not in class. All through the school day my thoughts wander, and I have to force myself to concentrate and complete my work before dismissal. On the way home I slow down while passing Jacob's house, trying to see without being obvious if he is at a window. I think I see a curtain stir, but no one is visible.

When I get home my mother and father are waiting, looking very serious. I know something is wrong.

My mother speaks first. "Hanna, go put your books away and change for your chores, then come down here. We need to have a word with you." My father, looking stern, only echoes her last words: "Yes, we need a word with you." As I climb the stairs a sense of dread fills me. A dozen reasons for this cross my mind. I have been so inordinately dishonest this last month and all of it has been so unlike me.

When I get down to the kitchen they have tea waiting for me, and in the middle of the table I see the note I passed to Jacob. Oh, damn.

My father begins this time. "Hanna, you are not a child anymore and we will not treat you like one. This is not a time for spankings or shouting. This is very serious and we must ask you to tell us what is going on."

My mother joins in. "As you can guess, Mr. and Mrs. Sparks came by today with this note. It is not signed, but Jacob told them it was from you and it does look like your handwriting. You disobeyed me. I am very disappointed in you. So, you must tell us why you wrote the note and *what* is going on."

I am found out. I have been betrayed by Jacob, either deliberately or by coercion, but betrayed. Yet I am strangely relieved. I look down at the note, which is opened and pressed flat, creases still showing.

> *"I have been forbidden to see you.*
> *We must be secretive.*
> *I have information to share with you.*
> *Can we meet after dinner tonight, 8 p.m.?*
> *On the corner? I'll be there. I hope you will."*

"Well, what have you to say? Is this the reason for your evening walk last night? How can we trust you after this? Are you seeing this boy? Do we need to be worried about anything? Because frankly, we are worried, we are worried sick about this. After the Sparkses came we could only sit and worry. We couldn't do the work we need to do. The cows need milking and we hope your sisters and brothers can do it this evening. The chickens need tending. What *were* you thinking?" This well-deserved rant from my mother is piling guilt upon guilt.

I sit down with them, feeling shaken. I try to compose myself and pour tea into my cup. "I'm sorry. I know I have disappointed you and I've disobeyed you. You may not understand this but I don't think that Diana killed herself, and neither does Jacob. We have been going about trying to get clues as to what happened. Jacob cared for her and did not break up with her as is the rumor. He did not break her heart so that she killed herself over it. We've just been trying to find out more. We've been trying to find out who may have influenced her or threatened her or maybe even killed her." I pause to take a sip of the hot sweet drink, then continue as both of my parents sit in silence watching me carefully. "I am not seeing Jacob, if you mean dating, that is. We have been meeting mostly at the library or for brief moments at school or sometimes on walks to talk about this. There is nothing going on between us besides that."

"*That* is a relief if we can believe you." This shot is from my mother. "But you know what his family is like. Yes, they are a well-to-do family, but many people don't respect them because of the conduct of Gilbert senior, and we've not heard good things about the two older boys, so we assumed that Jacob was just like them."

I nod. "Yes, I don't particularly like his brothers. They seem to be living up to their reputations, although I think that Edmund is not as bad as Gilbert junior. Jacob is not like them though, at least as far as I can determine. He actually seems their opposite. Diana had pretty good instincts about people and she thought he was a good person."

"So what is this about Diana? You think someone may have influenced her? You think some kind of crime was committed? Really? Aren't you being a bit dramatic?" This came from my father, an old-fashioned farmer who has no patience with drama.

"Well," I respond, "it may seem farfetched, but I don't think she killed herself. She had no reason to. It would be out of character for her to do that. I agree she seemed a bit troubled those last weeks before she died, but she never said anything to me that would lead me to believe that she had any reason to kill herself. I just don't think she did. So Jacob and I have been collaborating to find out more. We haven't found much so far." I don't want to tell them about breaking into the Turners' or about the note I found there.

My mother is next. "Well, we know you're concerned and that you're a good girl and wouldn't disobey or do these things without a good reason, so we want you to talk to Constable Cruthers. Maybe he can put your mind at ease. In the meantime, Jacob's parents don't want him socializing with you."

I interrupt. "But he's important to what we're trying to do…"

My mother continues, "Yes, they got pretty much the same information from Jacob that you've given us, but that is their wish. This is what we suggested to them, that if you are both so concerned, you should both meet with the constable. That way your meeting would be under the supervision of Constable Cruthers. They agreed." My mother watches my face to see my reaction.

I sip my tea, feeling relieved. "Okay, that is fair."

My mother has her dander up. "Really, I was insulted by the Sparkses. We are a good, honest, hard-working family. I feel like they are holding themselves above us, and I don't think they are any better than we are. That was why we proposed the compromise."

"Now," my father continues, "we don't want to hear your grades are slipping because you've been goofing off. We want you to get your chores done, and no more sneaking around. Okay?"

I nod. "Okay."

In many ways this is a great relief. My parents are wiser than most.

Chapter 16 – Constable Cruthers

The next day during lunch I walk to the town hall and speak to the town clerk, who says I can meet with the constable later after I get out of school. I can hardly contain myself and wonder if Constable Cruthers is willing to share any details of Diana's death with me.

After school I walk briskly down to the town hall to see the Constable who shares an office with several other town employees. I find myself wishing we had more privacy and when I mention that he kindly offers to find a private room for our talk. His looming hulk goes ahead of me down the hall to the town offices library, which is packed with filing cabinets and cardboard boxes overflowing with files. We sit down at a small table. The Constable pours himself coffee from a thermos and asks if I would care for some, but I decline. An evening light drifts in from the window over the table.

"Well, Hanna, I hear you've been doing some detective work." He looks directly at me at he sips his coffee.

"Where did you hear that?" I look at him in surprise. He tips his head to the side. "Don't you think I should be asking the questions?"

"Yes, but you will tell me, right?" He nods and I continue, "Diana was my friend, a good friend. I thought I knew her. I don't think she would have committed suicide, and she spent enough time down by the river to know how to be cautious. I don't think she would have accidentally fallen in either."

The constable watches me for a few seconds before responding. "Why didn't we talk about this when I first questioned you?"

"I'm not sure." I pause to think. "Maybe it was too fresh and I hadn't had time to think about it. Maybe I was in shock.

But now that I have had time to think it over, I doubt it was an accident." He nods again but stays silent, waiting for me to continue, so I add, "Jacob Sparks doesn't think so either." Now his eyebrows go up, the only sign he gives as he waits again for me to go on. "You know that Jacob was her boyfriend—well, as much of a boyfriend as she ever had. I don't know for sure if they even kissed, but he cared for her and she cared for him. I don't know why this worked—they were so different, she from a poor mill-worker's family and he from the mill supervisor's family. He was the one attracted to her. He thought she was something special, something out of his realm, something daringly exciting with her strange interests and wild ways. Diana said she thought that in the beginning he was interested in her only because it would bother his father, but after a while she realized he really did like her." I pause and the constable nods. "Go on," is all he says.

"So Jacob and I have been trying to understand why she would jump into the river, and we decided she wouldn't do that on her own. We've been looking for clues, looking for anything, and trying to get people to talk without being too obvious about it. Rumors, gossip—we've heard lots."

Finally Constable Cruthers says more than 'go on.' "So what did you find?"

"I was hoping we could share information. You know, you could tell me what you've found and I could tell you what we've found. But since I haven't seen Jacob in over a week I don't know if he's heard or found anything more." The constable scribbles something on the pad he brought with him, using a pencil on unlined paper.

"Hanna," he says in a patient tone, "you know I can't tell you what we've found. We cannot jeopardize the investigation."

"You mean," I say, surprised, "there is an investigation? Who else is working on this with you? Can you tell me that?"

"When anyone dies suspiciously, and suicide is considered a suspicious death, there is an investigation. There is a State Police detective working on this too. Of course it is not all that he does, but it is not just me investigating. I hope that puts your mind to rest."

"Well, yes, it does make me feel better." I do feel relieved that this is not going unnoticed and forgotten.

"So, what do you have to tell me?"

I hesitate. How much can I tell him? I don't want him to know that I broke into the Turners'. Maybe I could tell him that Jeffrey let me in and I picked up the papers then, but I want to finish the diary before I hand it over.

I start to tell him more about Diana and her interests and idiosyncrasies, and then I tell him about how some of the townspeople didn't like her. Then I tell him about the Sparkses and Gilbert junior, divulging some of what I found in the diary without telling him where it came from. I mention Billy, who harassed Diana in biology class. I say I think Jeffrey is a little odd. He nods at that and looks as though this confirms some things he knows. All the while he scribbles on the pad as I try to see from across the table what he's writing and what his handwriting looks like.

"What about Jacob? You said you thought he was a nice boy and that they were just friends?" The constable is starting to probe.

"Yes, I do think he's a nice boy, not like the other Sparks men, and as far as I know they were just friends. Diana, who shared a lot of secrets with me, never told me otherwise."

"Do you have anything else for me?" Again he asks this leading question. The light through the window is fading and the room is starting to get dark.

"I have something you should see. Can we go where there is brighter light?" He nods and gets up, leading me into his

83

shared office which is now empty; everyone else has gone home. The lamp over his desk throws a bright circle of light. He sits down, motioning me to sit across from him, and busies himself screwing the top back onto his thermos. I open my school book and take out the papers that Mr. Anders graded and start to explain what Jacob and I think about him. I tell Constable Cruthers about going into the house with Jeffrey and getting the papers and the quartz and the pen. I don't tell him about the diary.

Then I pause, trying to build the tension, and I slowly pull out the note and unfold it, opening it and pressing it flat on the desk in the circle of light. All the while I am watching him, looking for a reaction. He seems to blanch ever so slightly. He bends to examine it. "I found this in one of Diana's textbooks. What do you think it means and who could have written it?"

"You found this in one of her textbooks?" He picks it up gingerly by the corners and holds it up to the light. As he is scrutinizing it I try to get a better look at his notes. The handwriting is amazingly similar, the forward-leaning slant, the strongly crossed 't', the high flying dots on the 'i's' and the blunt ending to the words. He glances at me. I try to look innocent, raising my eyebrows.

"What do you think?" I ask. "Isn't this threatening? But who? Why?" I use my most innocent voice. He puts the note down and gives me a piercing look. "You found this when you went in with Jeffrey?" I nod. "We'll have to keep this as evidence." His voice is sterner now. I watch as he carefully places the note in a large envelope, which he writes on and puts in a file on the table behind his desk. I'm glad that I made a carbon copy of the original and can use it to see if I can find a match to the handwriting, maybe even to his. "Now," he says so loudly that it makes me start, "you should not be doing this investigating, you or Jacob. This is dangerous and you could be jeopardizing the case and putting yourselves in danger." I nod as he rises and looks as though he's getting ready to leave. "Go home. Don't get into any more mischief. Leave this investigation up to those of us who are professionals, okay?" I nod again, closing my book and getting up too. He puts on his coat. "I'm going to talk to Mr. and Mrs. Sparks so that they know what's going on, and while I think it's okay if you are friends with Jacob, no more of this detective work, hear?" I continue to nod. "I'm going to walk you part-way through the village. You should be safe from there, or do you want me to walk you home?"

"No, I'll be fine from there." I bundle up and go with him down the frozen gravel sidewalks towards my home. As we walk silently I am very conscious of this constable taking long strides beside me.

Once we get to the Sparks house he pauses and reminds me, "Remember, don't be doing any more of my work." At this he chuckles and I tell him I won't. He goes up the stone steps to the door as I continue towards home. I don't dare turn to look. I'm sure his is the same writing.

Chapter 17 – Fourth Entry – A Lie

Rather than thwarting my desire to find out what happened, the encounter with Constable Cruthers only makes me want to find out more. Can I trust my eyes? His handwriting is eerily similar to that on the note. Should I continue to check other handwriting? Who else's should I look at? Gilbert junior's? Jeffrey's?

When I get home, my parents, who knew I was to see the constable after school, ask me how the visit went. I tell them all that transpired except my suspicions about Constable Cruthers. I do not fail to add that he advised I could remain friends with Jacob and that he did not see any harm in that. My parents, taking it all in, say he is probably right and if Jacob's parents don't mind we can continue to study together, but we must follow the constable's advice and not do any more detective work. I am grateful for this and hope that his visit to the Sparkses will calm their fears of our becoming an investigative team so they will allow us to study together. But I really need to talk to Jacob. What happened at his home that resulted in the revealing of my note? And then his parents come to my house and confront my parents. Is this something Jacob did deliberately? Is he giving up our project? Has he found out things he doesn't want me to know? So many questions.

I begin to worry that he *is* somehow involved and that we are getting too close to his secret. Perhaps initially he worked with me knowing the investigation was going on and that it would be a way for him to steer suspicion away from himself or his creepy brothers. None of this will be answered until I can speak to him. Even then I think I no longer know if I can trust him to be honest with me. What if he is just a good liar, a good actor? How will I know? I've got to calm my mind, which is churning like our butter mill but nothing will solidify until I can get answers. I will try the diary again.

Diana Turner
April 15th, 1937

I can feel spring today. The air is delicious, the sun warm. I can finally smell the rich earth, not the hard and sterile snowbound winter ground. The tree buds are swelling and the willow branches have turned a chartreuse color. Maples are sending out their red and green blossoms. Peepers are chiming their million little bells and wood frogs croaking their hoarse bark. The spotted salamanders have migrated and already laid their globs of eggs in the swamp. And oh the birds! What raucous combinations of melodies and cries and silly flying to and fro looking for a mate and busily building nests. Turtles enjoy basking on a warm log after a long winter's sleep and plunk into the water if I go too close. I see raccoon footprints in the soft mud where they are searching for crawfish and mussels. The forest flowers, so delicate, are at their most elegant in the spring. They are not the showy and bold flowers of the summer fields but reveal their sweet shy faces only to those who are able to find them hidden in the leaves or among the lush ferns. The world is alive. I have thought, among my many silly thoughts, that if I could choose I would want to die in the springtime, for what a beautiful time it is.

Jacob is uncommonly sweet and follows me on walks to see the wonders of the springtime woods. We wade in the cold spring pools and I show him how to catch the crawfish by carefully coming up behind them and pressing them gently down so that they cannot reach back to grab you with their claws. He shows me how to catch a mermaid, he says, by lying on his back in a glade and caressing himself, until my desire intervenes. And oh, what a handsome and clever fisherman he is. Spring is indeed the time of love and beauty.

What do I care for the mean classmates, the cliques that shun me or the neighbors who are mean and bent on evil? I have spring and love to fill my cup and all the rest is meaningless.

Harry is sad when I leave him home for my Saturday jaunt with Jacob. Cecil follows but just watches quietly from the top of a nearby tree, no cawing, no crying. I will take Harry out every day next week to let him roam the warm spring woods and he will come back with mud up to his belly and dry leaves stuck in his hair. Springtime.

This entry shocks me. Both Diana and Jacob deny having any more than a friendship. What does this mean? Are they both lying to me? Can I trust Jacob? I feel betrayed by them both. I will watch him carefully and not let him know of my wariness or suspicions. I can trust no one.

Chapter 18 – Reconciled?

Jacob is in school the next day. I watch cautiously as he approaches me.

"Hi. We had a visit from Constable Cruthers last night. He spoke at length to my parents. Apparently he convinced them that we were friends and there was nothing to be alarmed about." He's friendly, relaxed, as though nothing has happened.

"Really?" I am amazed he is so nonchalant. "I had a talk with Constable Cruthers too," I say, my voice rising, "after your parents visited my house with the note *I gave you*." I cannot help but be angry.

Jacob leans back as if I'd slapped him.

"What happened?" he replies, in a tone that sounds sincerely surprised.

"You tell me what happened." I am trying to keep my voice down but the anger bleeds through my quiet tone. "For starters, how did your parents get that note?" I realize I'm poking his chest with my finger and I drop my hand. "Then you can tell me whose idea it was to get Cruthers involved. Was it your parents' idea or my parents'? Then—"

"Wait, wait," Jacob interrupts me. "When I got home from school Monday, the day I got your note, I was doing my homework and then I went down to supper. I think my father sneaked into my bedroom and found the note on my desk because when he came to the table he had it in his hand and confronted me with it. He guessed it was yours. I didn't tell him, but then he shouted and swore and called me some bad names and hit me. He's never hit me before. He told me I was a dolt for getting involved with cheap girls. That's when I snapped and said that neither you nor Diana were cheap girls. They told me I would have to stay in that night and not go out or call. I guess they visited your parents the next day and told them to keep you away from me. I don't know what happened after that but Cruthers came by last night."

"So why weren't you in school?" I can't fire questions fast enough.

"When my father hit me it left quite a mark. See?" He leans towards me and points at his cheek, which is a little discolored and has a small red gash. "I think my father didn't want people to know he hit me so they made the excuse that they needed to sort this all out and I was to stay home until it was resolved."

The bell is ringing and we will be late for class. "Can we talk later?" I ask. "I still have questions for you." He nods yes.

"Let's meet at the library after school. My parents said we could study together. I think they are afraid of a scandal and don't want to draw any more attention. You know everybody sees what's going on in this town."

At the library we claim the table we used before. The librarian nods at us as we pass, watches us all the way to the room and then pokes her head in when we are settled. I feel we are being spied upon. We open our books and start our homework, a plan we made as we walked over. We would be careful not to arouse suspicion and only when we were sure no one was close or listening would we break from our homework to talk about the last few weeks. After about fifteen minutes the postmaster comes in and asks for a particular book. Once the librarian finds it the postmaster goes to her desk and we can hear their low voices exchanging gossip.

I am anxious to talk while we have the chance. "So what else have you been up to? Have you discovered anything else?"

He pauses in his writing, gazing vacantly ahead as though trying to remember something, and looks quizzically at me. "What did you tell Cruthers?"

"I told him that, knowing Diana, we didn't think she would have committed suicide and that she was too agile and savvy about the river to fall in accidentally."

"But that wasn't all, was it? What else did you tell him? I heard my parents talking with him about some kind of note."

I am stuck. I am not yet ready to reveal to Jacob that I've been to Diana's, with and without Jeffrey. But now blabbermouth Cruthers has given up what I think is a valuable clue like it is nothing, and like it was his discovery. Damn that Cruthers. Or perhaps he is trying to flush someone out, trying to see what kind of reaction he will get from people. I wonder who else he went to. I wonder if he went to the Turners. Still, I don't like it. I don't like doing the dirty work and having someone else use it, and I want to know what other clues Cruthers has.

"What kind of relationship did you have with Diana? Really, were you just friends or was it more?" In changing the subject I totally turn the tables on him. I need to know if he is being honest with me or not.

"I told you we were friends. Don't you believe me?"

"Frankly, Jacob, I don't know what or who to believe anymore." That is the truth. We hear the library door close and the librarian walk past the door and we turn to our books, looking studious.

His head bent over his book, Jacob mumbles, "You don't trust me? My father hit me over *your* note. I came to you because I thought you would understand. That you, being her best friend, would understand that it probably wasn't an accident or a suicide. Why would I do that if I had anything to hide? It's been declared an accident, but a lot of people think it was a suicide. Either way, it does not implicate me. If I were guilty of anything, would I be looking into it further, stirring up trouble, or would I just let it all die down and be glad I got away with it?" He has a point. He continues, "I should take my parents' advice and just stay away from you."

"Listen, I'm sorry." I realize he might be my only ally in this. "I've gotten into trouble over it too."

"Maybe we should quit this like everyone wants us to." Jacob puts his hand over mine just as the librarian goes by. I can hear her pause at the door. We both pull our hands away and go back to our books and papers. She walks on and we both sigh in unison.

"I sure hope I can trust you," I say, "because I have a lot to tell you. When else can we get together? It's hard to talk here."

"Saturday. Meet me at the post office." I nod and we both settle in to finish up our homework as quickly as possible.

I am having another fitful night of. I can't sleep and go downstairs for a glass of milk.

My dreams are of water and darkness and pain. I awake again in a panic, gasping and cold.

Chapter 19 – Interesting

I am relieved to see Jacob waiting outside the post office. He walks up to meet me and points towards the road that passes my house. That makes me smile because it is the same road we walked the first time we met to talk. Once we are off the main road Jacob asks, "How are you doing?"

"I'm good. Some of my classes are getting harder and sometimes I have difficulty studying. My parents have been very good to me during all of this. They've listened and tried to understand. They don't know why I'm so obsessed with this. That is the exact word they used, obsessed. I don't have answers that satisfy them. I can only say what I think, what we both think. They try to understand, and they're being patient, but if I don't keep my grades up I'm afraid they'll lose their patience. So I must study harder."

"I know what you mean. My parents are worried too and harassing me to keep my grades up, and I have to work hard to get decent grades. It doesn't come easy to me. So, what do you have to tell me? What is the thing about the note the constable had?"

I am still torn; how much can I trust him? Although I know he is right, that he wouldn't be digging into this if he were guilty; he'd likely be lying low, not stirring things up. And I have to tell someone, and I have so much to tell. I deeply sigh and start out. "I have a lot to tell you, but you must promise, first, not to tell anyone, and second, not to judge me harshly. I have been driven to find out more and have gone to extremes I never would have imagined I would go to. I have told no one else, so if this gets out I will know you have been the person who betrayed my secrets."

Jacob stops, motions me to do the same, and faces me. "You are so serious. I know you are a decent person and an honest person, and a loyal friend. I cannot imagine anything so bad that it would shake my opinion of you." We were leaning against a large rock under a bare maple tree on the side of the road.

"I hope you are right," I say as I launch into my story. "A couple weeks ago I decided to try to get Diana's diary. I wanted to see if there were things going on in her life that she didn't tell me. I went down towards the mill on the path behind the Turners' knowing that Jeffrey would be using that path on his way home. I met him and talked him into letting me into her room to get her diary. We were going to do it the next Tuesday, after Mrs. Turner was to go into the village to work. He was going to take his morning break to meet me at the house. I had to fake illness to get out of school to meet him, which I did. We met and he let me into her room and I got the diary, and…" I hesitate and then start to cry. I can't help myself. I haven't told anyone about Jeffrey. I am ashamed and upset by it all over again.

"What happened? Did something happen?" Jacob sounds concerned, holding my wrist and watching my face. I start to tell the story in sobs that I'm sure are hard to understand.

Jacob is stunned. "He attacked you?" I nod, still sobbing. "That bastard! Are you okay? Did he hurt you?"

"I wasn't physically hurt, but I felt violated. I'm so ashamed."

"You haven't told anyone else about this?" I shake my head. "This is a terrible secret to keep. I'm sorry. I should have told you not to trust him, but I never expected you do that, to go to the house with him alone! Diana told me things about him, things she made me promise not to tell anyone." Jacob looks at me apologetically.

"You should have told me," I say. "We were working on this together. Didn't you think he could have been involved? Shouldn't you have said something earlier? We are supposed to be looking at everyone, right? Is there anything else you haven't told me? Anyone else you suspect?" I've gotten over being upset about the assault and am moving straight into indignation, wondering if he is keeping anything about his brothers from me too.

"Yeah, you're right. I should have told you about Jeffrey. Diana said he used to try to do things to her. I guess it started while they were younger. He would roughhouse with her and touch her in places that didn't seem right, but when you're wrestling it's hard to know what's accidental and what's not okay. Then later the horseplay became a lot more, you know, dirty. She never said how far it went, but it certainly was something that bothered her. That was one of the reasons she liked to be out of the house, and when she was home she stayed in the living room or went to her bedroom. She even put a hook on the inside of her bedroom door, but she suspected he sneaked in when she was out. She left things by her door so she could hear if he tried to, and Harry would bark and that would stop him. Damn. I should have told you, but I never suspected you would use him to get to her diary."

"Well, that's not the only thing you wouldn't suspect me of," I say with chagrin. "I went back when he wasn't around and broke into the house to see if I could find anything else." Jacob looks at me, eyebrows up, mouth open. "Oh, don't be so surprised. I'm not that much of a goody-two-shoes. Besides, I found some really interesting stuff."

"Have we now crossed over to being criminals in trying to get at the facts?" Jacob is still incredulous.

"Not we. Only me. As far as I know I'm the only one doing things that are illegal, unless there are things you haven't told me." Jacob shakes his head. His expression tells me he's not sure if this alliance is wise. "Oh, stop looking at me like that. You're no angel, are you?" Now his expression is even stranger but I ignore him.

"Listen, this is what I found. Remember that note that Cruthers had? Well, *I* found it. When I went back that second time I found it in a bunch of papers. Most of the papers were schoolwork. Schoolwork graded by Mr. Anders, who thought she was a brilliant student. Maybe he was trying to manipulate her; I'm not sure. I don't know if there was anything more between them. But I found a note. It was written in longhand with a pencil on an unlined piece of paper. I compared the handwriting to everything I could find of Mr. Anders's, but it didn't look the same. We need handwriting notes from everyone, from Jeffrey, from Gilbert, from…"

"Hold on." Jacob stops me. "You suspect Gilbert?"

"I suspect everyone. Even you." Jacob leans back and looks angry. "You still suspect me?"

"No, no," I try to smooth it over. "I'm just trying to get you to realize it could have been anyone, anyone but you and me."

"Well, what did the note say?"

"It said, 'Tell him he had better leave you alone or I will KILL HIM!' That was exactly what it said. Who wrote it or who they were threatening I don't know."

Jacob looks down, concentrating, then back at me.

"What happened to the note? Is that the one that Cruthers has?"

"Yes. My parents insisted that I see him or they wouldn't let me go out. I would have been almost a prisoner in my home. So I went down and talked to him. I told him almost everything—well, except finding the diary and breaking into the house. He said the investigation was ongoing. I really thought he could help. Then he took the note and said he would look into it further. But here is the strange part. While I was there he was taking notes, taking them on unlined paper with a pencil in longhand, and the writing in the note I gave him looked a lot like his handwriting. When he was first taking the notes he was relaxed until he caught me watching him, and then he got tense and seemed to shorten our meeting. I was somewhat frightened, but he let me go and I haven't seen him since. So I don't have the note, but I made a carbon copy that I have at home. What do you think? Can we get other people's handwriting?"

Jacob is serious. "You saw the handwriting and you thought it looked like his?" I nod. "And," I add, "it was really creepy the way he acted after he caught me watching him."

"We could get into a lot of trouble if they knew we were still talking about this, still thinking about investigating more," Jacob warns. "And everyone is watching—our parents, probably the librarian, Cruthers, and who knows who else. If we're going to go further we have to be very careful. I'm not even sure if we should."

I look at him, realizing that even though this is important and we should be trying to figure it out we could be getting ourselves into a lot of trouble. "But that's just what they want, or someone wants. They want us to drop it."

"So," Jacob says, "you don't think the investigators are doing a good job and we could do better?"

"I guess I am saying that. I mean, I found the note, and the diary. Shouldn't they have looked for evidence like that and found it? Are they really investigating or are they just letting the file sit on their desks, waiting for the trail to get cold?"

"I'm afraid that we'll get caught." Jacob is nervous and I think he's trying to back out.

"Well, I won't let this go until I know what happened. You can either help me, or drop it and keep my secret, whichever you choose." I am losing patience with his anxiety.

"Listen, I'm just trying to be sensible. I didn't say I thought we should stop. I just want you to think about it, think of the consequences. Factor them into your plan. Maybe we have to take steps to throw them off."

"What do you mean?" I think I hear a strange tone in his voice.

"You know, we can do things to make them think we're not up to what we are up to."

"Okay?" I'm still not getting it.

"Pretend we're dating." He looks at me as though I am a dunce.

"Oh." I'm sure there is a small element of surprise in my voice. Why hadn't that occurred to me? And it's interesting that it did occur to Jacob. "That's a pretty good idea if we can pull it off and not get our parents upset."

"Good. I'm glad we agree." Jacob sounds relieved. "But right now we've got to get back. We've been away too long and people will start to wonder where we are." He pauses, looking skyward as though compiling a list in his head. "This is my suggestion. We need to keep our stories straight. We shouldn't say anything about where we were or what we've been doing without checking with each other first. We don't want to give conflicting stories that people can check. Like today we should say the obvious, that we've been out for a walk together. Probably we should stick to our routine, meet at the library and go for a walk now and then, so we shouldn't have to fabricate too much. I can't wait to see you again. I'm very interested in the diary. Can you bring it?"

"I don't think that's a good idea." I'm thinking about the last entry I read and I want to read more before I start sharing it. "I'll keep reading it and tell you what I find as I go along."

He nods okay as he starts back. "Let's get going, and I'll see you Monday after school at the library?"

"Yeah, that sounds good." We walk in silence down the hill towards the village.

For the first time in weeks I get a good night's sleep.

Chapter 20 – Entries Five and Six

After dinner on Saturday I study until I fall asleep on my books. Sunday is busy with church and then chores that keep me working until supper. I am tired. Farming doesn't take a Sunday break. Beasts always need tending, food needs putting up. Winter or summer, it doesn't matter—weekdays or weekends, there is always work to be done on a farm.

So Sunday night after I finish I go up to my bedroom with the excuse that I need to read a book for a report. I climb into bed with my book but I also have the diary under the covers. I read the book but pull the diary out when I know no one is coming and read as much as I can before I have to hide it and go back to my book. In this way I am able to get through several entries in the diary.

Diana Turner
April 20th, 1937

I can write now. I can write more freely than I could before. I can tell you things that I was afraid to write before because I thought someone was reading this. I now know that was true—someone was reading it. I found this out when I wrote misleading entries and was confronted over them. Now I carry it with me; my diary goes to school and comes home with me and I hide it carefully when I get home.

It is Jeffrey. He has been bothering me. He was reading my diary. I wasn't sure of it until I wrote something in it that was not true. I wrote something about us - about Jacob and me. The next day Jeffrey confronted me. He told me he was going to tell our parents. He was very aggressive. He said I shouldn't be doing things with Jacob, that it wasn't right, that I was too young. He was acting very protective. But I knew it was because he was jealous. He was jealous of Jacob, of what he thought we were doing. He told me we had to stop. He said I was supposed to save myself for my husband. I thought that was an odd thing for him to say. In the past he has been too physically friendly with me. I am always wary of him. I'm wary of being in the house alone with him, which I never allow myself to be. Harry intuitively knows that the brother and sister attachment is strained and that I am uncomfortable with Jeffrey. Harry watches and sleeps by my bed and if the door makes a noise after I put the latch on it at night, Harry gives out a low growl which wakes me and sends the sly brother of mine away.

Jacob is good and listens when I tell him about Jeffrey. He is concerned, but there is little he can do. I cannot tell anyone else. My father and mother worship Jeffrey. I don't think they would believe me if I told them what went on. They would probably say it was my imagination, that it wasn't what Jeffrey was about at all. He has manipulated them so.

I'm going to work at the mill this summer. Papa said I could and I need some money. Poor Harry and Cecil get only little scraps of food and the cats subsist mainly on mice and other small critters. Sometimes when Hanna sends me home with milk I pour a little out for them – what a treat!

I doubt that the mill work will be fun. There are few women there except in the office and I don't have office skills. I'm sure Mr. Sparks will be keeping me on my toes. But as long as Gilbert junior doesn't come by the mill, I should be all right there.

Harry is my sweet pup. He cut his footpad yesterday when we were walking by the river. I think someone broke a beer bottle and left it there. The fishermen are often just pigs, leaving behind cans of old dead worms and beer bottles and whatever else they can't be bothered to bring home. Sometimes they clean the fish there and discard the entrails, though that is not much of a problem because there are always scavengers willing to make a meal of those leavings.

So now I write when I can and then carefully hide my diary. Harry protects me and my parents do not. Odd, isn't it?

Diana Turner
April 28th, 1937

Mr. Anders took me aside today and said that he needed to talk to me. At first I was nervous, but when I went to see him he was very kind. You won't believe what he wanted to tell me. He said that he and his wife had never had children and that he had talked to her and that if I was interested he thought he could get me into a college when I graduate! Can you believe that? He said his wife was very excited about it as he had been telling her about me and showing her my papers. He said she is a schoolteacher too and gets excited about gifted students. He said I would still have to come up with some of the money, but with their help I might be able to get a grant too. What would I be? A biologist? A teacher? I am excited beyond words! He said I would have to bring some of my other grades up. I need to work on math and to improve my English, which is not the best. I'm going to college!!!!

Goodness. Mr. Anders? I never knew. I never heard her talk about it.

Now I know what happened with the other diary entry with Jacob. It wasn't real. It was something Diana fabricated to flush out her sly brother. How awful. It's not enough that he's harassing her and she feels uncomfortable in her own home, but her parents think so much of their son that they ignore their daughter and her needs and safety. What kind of parents are these? I feel so lucky in my home with my family. If one of my brothers were to bother me I know my parents would listen to me. They would listen to both of us. What wonderful, even-handed parents. But I have to wonder how many people live like Diana, where the girls in the family are not encouraged, protected or even believed.

I am much relieved to find that Jacob was telling me the truth about his relationship with Diana. Now I'm sure he is someone I can trust and confide in.

Chapter 21 – Mr. Anders

I'm back at school, and every moment when I am not studying I am thinking about our investigation. That's what I've decided to call it privately, an investigation. But I know I must keep it all quiet so I only call it that with Jacob. I've decided I might try to approach Mr. Anders and see what he has to say. Since I think his handwriting does not match that of the note, at least he is not guilty of writing that. He also seemed genuinely interested in helping Diana. I think he is not a suspect.

After school I stop by his classroom.

"Hi, Mr. Anders. Do you have a minute?"

He is sitting at his desk shuffling through some papers. "Hello, Hanna. Sure, I've got a few minutes. Come on in."

I go in and pull up a chair near his desk. He looks surprised and says, "Well, is this a long visit?" I laugh. "No, not too long. I just have a couple questions."

He nods. "Okay, what do you need?"

"I wanted to talk to you about Diana." I see his face get pinched as he takes his glasses off and presses his finger on the bridge of his nose. Then he takes out his handkerchief, blows his nose, wipes his eyes, pauses, and puts his glasses back on. "Excuse me. I'm still saddened by her loss. I know she was a good friend of yours. I'm sorry for your loss too." Suddenly I find myself tearing up. I wasn't expecting this. I sniff and thank him.

I don't have time to be vague; I come right to the point. "I know that you liked Diana. I know you thought she was a special student and that you tried to help her. Did anything happen in those last months that made you think something was wrong?"

Mr. Anders looks hard at me. "Do you think there was something wrong?" He has turned the question around to me.

"Yes. I thought she was acting very oddly toward the end, but before that, what happened? What happened to make her get so strange? Do you think was there something that upset her?"

Mr. Anders is nodding. "Yes, I thought she was acting strangely too." He pauses, thinking. "This past spring I was talking to her about college. I thought she had a good chance to get in if she studied hard and brought her other grades up. My wife and I even agreed to help her. But her parents didn't like it and told her she couldn't do it, that they wouldn't give her their permission. We thought she really didn't need their permission to go. And we couldn't understand why they would deny her the chance to go to college. Though we were disheartened we still encouraged her, but we think it set her on a downward spiral. I think just having her parents not believe in her upset and depressed her."

"Wow. Really? Why would they do that?"

Mr. Anders shakes his head. "I don't know."

"Is there anything else you noticed or thought was strange? Were there people in class who were bothering her? I thought she had a little trouble with one of her classmates last year."

"Oh, yes, you mean Billy. No, he was just a smart aleck. He really didn't mean anything. I think he just wanted to get her attention. I think he was harmless, and he stopped after a few weeks. Other than that I can't think of anyone who was really bothering her. You know she was a character and acted tough, so most of the time people didn't usually bother her much. Sometimes when we talked I told her not to be so 'bristly,' that by being abrasive she kept away people who could be her friends. But I don't think she trusted most people. Maybe she thought they weren't sincere. Maybe she thought they didn't like her, but if she had tried she probably could have had more friends. I miss her. She had a quick and original mind."

"I miss her too," I say. "Thank you for your time, and if you think of anything else would you let me know?" He nods as I get up, put the chair back, and head to my meeting with Jacob.

The library is busier than usual. Two other people are in the quiet room that we are usually able to have to ourselves. It is a pretty room, round like a castle turret with windows all around above the bookcases. There is a large table near the windows and a smaller one closer to the door. Jacob is seated where we usually sit at the larger table. He looks up expectantly when I walk in and moves some papers away from the chair I pull out.

"You'll never guess where I've just come from," I say, hoping to sound mysterious and tantalizing.

"Mr. Anders's office?" he offers with a tiny smile.

"You saw me, didn't you?" He nods.

"Well, did you know that Mr. Anders offered to pay for Diana to go to college?" Now I get the effect I want: his eyebrows shoot up and he leans back in the chair. "Really? He told you that?" I nod.

"I need to tell you about the diary. I've only read about five or six entries, but they tell a lot." I tell him about the first entry, how she is so angry and dislikes the town and small-town life and her sad lot in it. In the second entry she talks about Jacob and then about Gilbert junior trying to kiss her. Then the third entry is about how dismal and cold her house is and how she values her animal friends and Jacob. I tell him about the fourth entry when she writes misleadingly about herself and Jacob making love in the woods.

"Stop! Stop! That didn't happen!" Jacob says this loudly and the other people in the room turn to look at us.

"I know, I know, but there is a reason she wrote it. In the next entry she reveals she believes someone is reading her diary, and she knows it's Jeffrey when he confronts her about you and she having an affair. So she starts carrying the diary to school with her and hiding it when she's home. She put a latch on her door and kept Harry close so Jeffrey wouldn't sneak into her room while she was asleep. It is so depressing because she didn't feel she could tell her parents how he was. She thought they would not believe her."

Jacob nods. "I know. She told me about how they thought Jeffrey was perfect and how little they thought of her. I always felt bad for her too. I know what it's like to be the least favorite child always trying to live up to the other brothers' perfections. Not that they were perfect, but from my parents' perspective they may as well have been."

"So let me tell you about the last two entries that I read. Diana starts carrying the diary around with her and Jeffrey is bothering her. Then she talks about planning to start work at the mill and about Mr. Anders offering to help with college. I can't wait to read the next entry—who knows what's in it? But since Mr. Anders has already said the Turners wouldn't let him send Diana to college, it's probably not good." Jacob nods understandingly.

"I'll get the diary to you as soon as I finish it, okay? I think you'll like reading it. You must understand that these are her most private thoughts so you have to treat it with respect and with the knowledge that she did not expect anyone else to read it. So don't be surprised by what's in it."

"I had no idea Gilbert had harassed Diana. That puts him in a different light. I think maybe we should get a sample of his handwriting—you know, just in case." I am glad to see Jacob is coming around to my way of thinking.

We both settle down to serious studying.

Chapter 22 – Grace

We have narrowed down the list of suspects to three: Jeffrey, Gilbert junior and Constable Cruthers. I am writing down and evaluating all I know about each man.

As her brother Jeffry had a lot of access to Diana, knowing where she was and what she was doing much of the time. He was known to prey on her. He was able to sway his parents against her, perhaps creating in her a fear which led to her accident. He may have been jealous of Jacob. He knows the woods behind their house and down by the river as well as Diana did. He also seems unpredictable.

Gilbert junior, Jacob's brother, is someone I would not trust. I have not had any personal contact with him but from what I've heard and read, he's someone to avoid. I don't think he has a high regard for women. He drinks too much at times, or so Jacob says, and Jacob thinks he loses control when he does. We should definitely watch him. I hope this does not offend Jacob.

To me Cruthers is the most frightening. Why do I suspect him? First of all, because he has all the details of the case he can manipulate them to suit his needs. It would be easy for him to cover up facts or clues that would otherwise point at him, or someone else. His suspicious actions after he thought I'd been watching him write his notes was very significant to me. His handwriting was quite similar to the writing on the note. Because he has the power and influence to shut down our activity. We must be very stealthy. He likely knows more about what is going on in this town than anyone else, including the postmaster, the market owner and the librarian. Of all the suspects, he is the most dangerous.

Our plan is to eliminate them as suspects one by one, but which should we start with? The least likely to be guilty should be the easiest one to eliminate. I think we need to check out Gilbert junior first, mostly because focusing on Cruthers is daunting. Jacob will get a copy of Gilbert's handwriting.

But I have to admit, finding out who wrote the note does not necessarily mean we have found the person responsible. We don't yet know what the note means. Obviously someone was either jealous or protective of Diana, but that doesn't mean he is implicated. It could be that someone just wanted to scare Diana into being safe. But saying you will "KILL HIM" is a very frightening threat. Who would write such a menacing message?

So as I think about it I almost talk myself out of using the note to implicate whoever wrote it. But I have come up with another plan to see if Gilbert junior had anything to do with it. It is far-fetched, just the kind of plan Diana would approve of. I can't wait to talk to Jacob to see if he likes it.

When we meet at the library no one is in our room. I start to frame my plan by listing our suspects and the reasons to eliminate the least likely first. I also give Jacob my thoughts about the note and how valid or invalid it could prove in our search. Then I lay out my plan to discover if Gilbert junior was involved.

"I know this is kind of wild, but I think it will work. The biggest problem is that it will require enlisting my sister Grace, who isn't always easy to deal with. But something as crazy as this might appeal to her. As long as she can keep her mouth shut and not tell my parents, we'll be safe." I'm excited as I continue to explain my idea. "I know from what you've told me that Gilbert junior likes to drink, and he gets drunk at times, right?" Jacob nods. "I think we should have Grace meet him in the tavern at Sherman's Corner, help him get drunk and then try to get him to talk. People who are inebriated tend to talk with less discretion. If

110

Grace knew what to say and how to say it, we might be able to get him to trip up." Jacob is shaking his head.

"I think that is a crazy idea. What if he is able to get Grace out of there? He could hurt her. What if it just doesn't work and he doesn't say anything?"

I have thought of this too. "Well, we should be at the tavern in case he tries to take Grace out. And if he doesn't say anything, we are in no worse a position than we are now. But what if he does let some things slip? What then?"

"It's all so daft." Jacob is stating the obvious.

"Yes, it is, and that's why it might work. If— if I can get my sister to go along with it, if I tell her why and what we're trying to do, I bet she will. She's not the fraidy cat she sometimes seems like."

"Well, I guess we could try it. What *do* we have to lose? You'll talk to your sister? What if she turns on you? We'll be in trouble again."

"I know, but I'm hoping it will work and Grace will be willing. I'll see if I can get a chance to ask her tonight. Maybe she can do it this weekend. She could meet him in the back of the little tavern, right? It opens after the gas station shuts down, I think. That would be perfect."

Jacob is nodding. "Yeah, I think I've heard him talking about it, about meeting friends down there. Sometimes I hear him come in at 1 a.m. when he stumbles up the stairs. If he's waking our parents they're not saying anything. You know, Gilbert junior can do no wrong." Jacob sounds disgusted and hurt by his parents' favoritism.

I find the perfect chance that evening after dinner. Grace goes upstairs to start her homework and Ida is still doing dishes. I go upstairs and sit across from Grace and approach the subject very carefully, so that perhaps if I phrase it right I won't get in trouble if she balks.

"Grace, I want to ask you something and I hope you'll be understanding about it." Grace puts down her pen and looks at me. "I think that something bad happened to Diana." She stares at me and her eyebrows go up. "You know that Jacob and I have been trying to find out what happened." She nods. "Well, we think that Gilbert junior, Jacob's brother, may be involved."

"So what does that have to do with me?" She has a tone, but I continue calmly. "We want to see if we can get him to talk and we were hoping you would help us." I can see storm clouds starting to gather on her brow. "Listen, please don't tell Mom and Dad. I'm in enough trouble already. But both Jacob and I think that with your help we can either prove or disprove his guilt." She just continues to stare, but the storm clouds lessen a little. "This is what we want you to do. Take Gilbert out to Sherman's Corner this weekend. Tell him you want to meet him there for a beer. When you get there, let him drink lots; you know he can be a heavy drinker. Then see if you can get him talking. Ask him about Diana and see if he says anything. Maybe he'll just start talking. If he doesn't, or he acts guilty, wait a few minutes and then say, 'I know what you did.' Don't say anything more than that and see how he reacts. Watch to see if he seems guilty or nervous or uncomfortable. If not, repeat it a little later, and see what he does and what he says. We know this is a long shot, but it may work to get some information."

"You know," Grace replies, seriously, "I could get into real trouble for this and I'm not even supposed to be drinking yet. If Mom and Dad hear about it I would really be in trouble myself." I nod. "Yes, I certainly wouldn't say anything, and if you can find a remote booth in the back, no one we know should see you."

Grace smiles a half smile, looking kind of mischievous. "Let me think about it. I won't tell Mom and Dad, but you should be careful or you will get into a world of trouble."

"I know." And I do know. I also know that I gauged Grace correctly. She has a daring side that most people never see.

Chapter 23 – Gilbert Junior

Jacob and I thought we would have trouble getting into the tavern at Sherman's Corner. We tell them we only want sodas and hamburgers and they finally allow us in. The waitress leads us away from other tables to the far back corner by the small dance floor. I guess they don't want anyone complaining about kids in the bar. This is to our advantage as we only want to see what is going on. We get there about twenty minutes before we expect Grace and Gilbert to arrive. We settle down with our sodas and then order French fries. We each have a school book and we try to look inconspicuous sitting there reading. We are trying to focus on our books and not look at the few diners back in our area, some of whom are eyeing us with curiosity.

Finally the two of them come in. Gilbert casually directs Grace into a booth that fortunately is out of our direct view. When a waiter goes to their booth Gilbert orders a couple beers. The waiter seems friendly with Gilbert, who must be a good customer because they don't ask how old Grace is or if it is okay to serve her alcohol.

There are several other couples in the room and several more coming. The low windows near some of the booths have dull red curtains that look greasy. The booths without windows are dark until a waiter comes around with candles in red glass jars, which he lights and puts into the booths and on the other tables. Towards the front of the room in the center is a large rectangular bar with stools all around. A couple of men sit there looking like it is their personal and permanent real estate. In the front window a red neon sign buzzes BEER backwards, so passers-by on the street can read it. A large woodstove in one corner is stoked and the fire pops and crackles. Several couples have chosen to sit close to this black-and-chrome beast. A metal pipe railing around it keeps the customers at a safe distance. We have plenty of time to take all this in while Gilbert and Grace are consuming their first round.

Grace knew she wouldn't be able to keep up with Gilbert's beer consumption. She had an ingenious idea to get rid of most of her beer, taking only a few well-spaced-out sips from each round. She has brought a hot water bottle in her handbag, into which she carefully dumps beer when Gilbert isn't looking. She opens her bag out of view below the table, pours in beer and then raises the glass to her lips as though she has just had a sip. Gilbert is busy talking to chums about himself and his exploits so he does not notice Grace's act. After a while she will go to the ladies room and presumably dump the contents of the hot water bottle into the sink. Grace is really into this. Gilbert keeps drinking. We have to admit he is good at holding his alcohol. We sit for nearly two hours waiting for something to happen, for either one of them to leave. We dilly-dally, ordering burgers and more sodas. We are trying to eat slowly so the waiter won't want us to give up our booth, although there are not that many people in the place. Finally, after an untold number of beers Gilbert gets up and goes to the bathroom. Grace hurries back to our booth.

"What are you doing here? He might see you. I didn't know you were going to be here," Grace hisses nervously.

"We were worried about you. What if he gets weird and tries to drag you outside? There's a side door right behind your booth."

"Okay, but don't move around. He's starting to get loose, talking about his parents, talking about you, Jacob. I think he's almost ready. I've got to get back. If I leave, don't leave at the same time unless he follows me." We nod and Grace walks quickly back to the booth to empty more beer into her bag.

Gilbert finally comes out of the men's room, walking unsteadily towards the booth. He bounces off a table and turns to look at it as though wondering why it suddenly appeared in front of him. We both snicker quietly. "Boy," Jacob said under his breath, "if my parents could see him now…"

After another half hour or so Grace gets up and puts on her coat. We can hear her say, "Well, I've got to get home. I told my parents I'd be back by nine." We see Gilbert lean out and grab her wrist.

"Oh come on, you can stay a little longer. We just got started. You haven't told me anything about your family. Come on." He has a wheedling tone, patting the bench beside him. Then he switches to sarcasm. "What are you afraid of? Afraid of your parents, little girl?" I know that will annoy Grace.

"Listen," she says firmly, "you're drunk and I'm bored and I'm going home." She finishes pulling on her coat and gloves and turns towards the door

"You're a prick-tease, Grace Smith," are the last words Gilbert junior throws after her as she leaves. We wait expectantly. Is he going to follow her? But he just sits there for a minute, finishing off his beer before moving to the bar, sliding onto a stool and ordering another. He buys a pack of cigarettes and lights one, blowing the smoke up into the lights above the bar.

We decide it is time to go. We leave some cash at the booth and slip out the side door.

It is after nine and we still have a mile-long walk home. After the hours in the tavern surrounded by the odor of spilled beer and stale cigarette smoke and an occasional faint whiff of urine and vomit, the air outside smells delightfully fresh and clean.

We walk briskly, hoping to catch up to Grace, but she must have been so glad to get away that she ran home.

We part at the turnoff to my house, shaking hands because we successfully evaded detection. Now I will find out what Gilbert said. I can't wait to get home.

I breeze through the house to our bedroom. Grace is dressing for bed. She looks at me as I come in. "I need to get some studying done. Will you do some of my chores for me tomorrow?"

"Of course," I reply

Ida wakes up. "What are you two doing up and where have you been?"

"Oh, don't worry. Just go to sleep, Ida." Grace, not to be prodded, slips into bed with Ida, who is already asleep again and rolls over with a snorting snore.

"When can we talk?" I am anxious.

"Not tonight. I'm tired. But I have some interesting stuff to tell you."

"Oh," I whisper, exasperated. "You *are* a tease."

I can hear her chuckle.

In the morning Grace surprises me by offering to milk one of the cows, prodding me to go with her and milk one of the others. Breakfast is almost on the table but she says we should be back in about twenty minutes. We each grab a milking bucket and another with warm water and a rag and head out to the barn.

The two easiest milkers are next to each other. We wash their teats and sit down. "I'll tell you," Grace starts, "that is one self-centered fellow. He talked about himself and his school chums for at least an hour, but then as he became more inebriated he started to whine about his parents, who he thinks expect too much of him because he's the oldest. Then he whined about Jacob, who as the 'baby' got away with too much and wasn't interested in moving up in the world."

"Yeah," I say. I can hear her clearly over the rhythmic squish, squish, squish of milk squirting into the buckets. My face is leaning against the warm side of the cow. Grace continues. "When I said, 'It's too bad about Diana, isn't it?' his head snapped up. 'She was another tease. You should see how she was stringing my brother along. He's such a dunce. What the hell did he see in her?' I watched him with disgust. He is such a troll. Then I asked him if he thought her death was an accident and he gave me the weirdest look. Really, it gave me the creeps when he curled his lip and said, 'If it wasn't an accident, she got what she had coming.' I asked him what he meant and he said, 'Like I said, she was a tease. She teased enough guys around town and it probably just caught up with her.' When I said I thought she wasn't that bad he added, 'And she was weird, you know, trousers and all that sneaking through the woods—it was unnatural for a girl. Witchy. But it all came back to get her, didn't it?' That's when I tried to change the subject, and then shortly after I left."

"Wow. So what do you think?" I ask this believing I already know what she will answer.

"I don't think he had anything to do with it. He's a jerk, and he didn't like her, but I don't think he was involved."

"Yeah, it doesn't sound like it. Thanks, Sis. I owe you."

"Don't worry, you'll be making up for it. You've got my pot duty for a week."

"Okay, that's fair."

"But you know what?" She pauses. "I thought it was fun, except that I don't like him. What other people are you suspicious of? You can tell me now; I'm in on it."

"Okay, but please don't tell Mom and Dad."

"Of course not. I'm in this too now."

"Well, Jeffrey is one, and don't be shocked, but we're also suspicious of Constable Cruthers."

"Really?" Grace does sound shocked.

"In the beginning we thought Mr. Anders might be a suspect, but you know what? He turned out to be a really nice guy who was trying to help Diana. So we're pretty sure now he wasn't involved."

We finish up our milking and head back to the house.

"Remember," Grace reminds me, "you're doing my pots and pans for the week."

Chapter 24 – The Cruthers

After I tell Jacob what Grace had to say, we pretty much rule out Gilbert junior and we need to focus on someone else. Jacob is disturbed to hear that his brother is imagining himself to be the stressed older brother carrying the heavy weight of responsibility. "What a laugh. He's whining about his tough life to a girl in a bar as he proceeds to get drunk. I am so happy I don't follow him as a role model. I cannot think of a poorer example."

"I agree," I reply. "He is not someone who commands respect, but I don't think he was involved." Jacob shakes his head. "No, I agree, he's guilty only of being a jerk."

"So ruling him out leaves just two other suspects, at least only two so far. I suppose there could be others. We will just have to keep looking and listening." I want to focus on our next step. "What do we do now?"

Jacob gives me a thoughtful look. "I'll tell you what I think. I think we need to find out more about Cruthers."

"Yeah, I guess so. I hope we find something soon. I'm beginning to feel like we're wasting time. Maybe it really was an accident, or maybe she did it deliberately."

Jacob is losing patience. "You don't really believe that. You're just tired of all this chasing around and being suspicious of everyone. It takes a lot of energy to be vigilant all the time. It's hard to suspect people we've always respected. And then during the process of looking for evidence we find out things that surprise us, like discovering Mr. Anders is a good guy after thinking bad things about him. Or finding out how much of a jerk my brother really is. I'm beginning to question my judgment. So many people aren't really who they appear to be."

I need to make a decision before Jacob loses his will to keep going. "I'm going to visit Cruthers tomorrow and ask him if he's found out anything more, just to see how he reacts. I would appreciate it if you'd wait for me at the library just in case. If I don't get there by 5:30, go looking for me at Cruthers's office, okay?" Jacob is a little apprehensive about this, but agrees to wait for me.

I am nervous as I enter the constable's office. Several others are still at their desks and they watch me as I come in. Cruthers is working, bent low over paperwork, so focused that he doesn't hear me approach until I gently knock on his desk to get his attention. He starts, sits up straight and glares at me.

"Sorry. I didn't mean to startle you."

He recovers, offers a thin-lipped smile, and says in a voice that is less than welcoming, "That's all right, Hanna. What can I do for you?" Everyone is watching the interaction.

"I know you're busy and I don't want to take up too much of your time, but I was just curious about the case. Actually I have a little information that just— well, someone told me. Can we talk for a minute?"

I can feel the people around us listening to our every word. Even if they look like they were working, I know they are taking everything in.

"Well," Constable Cruthers answers, sounding official, "this is highly irregular. You know I can't share details of a case with a member of the public." I nod. "But," he continues, "if you have some information for me I would certainly want to know what it is." Picking up the notepad and pencil he says, "Why don't we just go somewhere a little more private?" He leads me into the town office library again, which seems even more crammed with boxes of files than last time I was here. This time he hasn't brought his coffee.

With the pad he motions me to sit down at the table, and he sits down opposite. Putting the pad on the table he leans forward and asks, "So, what do you have for me?"

I fidget. In my mind things played out differently. In my mind he's the one who is nervous and fidgeting. "Well, we've been watching Gilbert junior…" Constable Cruthers interrupts. "Gilbert junior certainly is a troublemaker, and has gotten into trouble before. Why, if it weren't for his father he would have been arrested."

I'm sure this is not something the Constable should be sharing with me, but I take advantage of it. "Well, he almost got into trouble again."

"What has he done? What do you know?" Cruthers is getting right on it.

"He went out with my sister the other night and got himself drunk and was buying drinks for her, and she's underage you know."

"Your sister is a fool to go out with that one. You tell her she should stay away from him. He's already gotten two girls in the county into trouble. It caused a real ruckus. The only thing that kept the families from filing lawsuits was his father forking out some cash. He's nothing but a bum, and he's got a father who's powerful in local politics so that makes him a dangerous bum. Those girls' lives were ruined. They were good girls from good families, but they got mesmerized by his sweet talk. Is that all you have for me? Gilbert junior being himself?" I nod. "Well, just tell your sister to stay away from him. Sooner or later he'll get himself into real trouble that his daddy can't get him out of and then he won't be my problem anymore. To get back to what you're really interested in: I don't think Gilbert had anything to do with Diana's death, but I won't totally rule him out yet."

I am surprised at how much he is telling me. I have to ask myself again, Are we looking at all the wrong people? I venture a question. "What about Jeffrey?"

He squints at me. "You are awfully curious for someone who isn't supposed to be doing her own investigation. But I'll tell you this, he is still a suspect. And that is all I can tell you." He gets up, picking up the pad. "Now get home. You're not supposed to be doing this and I don't want you to be endangering yourself or causing the townsfolk to get all worked up because you're asking too many questions. But if you hear anything else, come on down." He winks at me and points towards the door.

Am I again misjudging someone? He has just opened up about Gilbert junior and I had hardly said anything. Gilbert must be a real thorn in his side. How do you enforce the law, tell parents to watch their kids, and not have the parents or the kids mad at you and causing you more trouble? It's got to be hard. And here we are two teenagers, out messing with things that should be his domain. What if we screw up his investigation? I am beginning to like Cruthers. But I am not going to throw him into the Not Guilty bucket yet. I am going to watch him.

I get to the library around 5:00. Jacob is there and smiles when I come in. "Whew. I'm glad you're here. I didn't want to have to save you from Cruthers. So what did you find out? Anything?"

As I sit down I notice someone at the other table. "Well," I lean forward and whisper, "he doesn't think much of your brother. Cruthers says he's going to get himself into real trouble one of these days." I lean back, opening my book. "I asked him about Jeffrey and all he said was that he is still a suspect." I page through to the chapter we are studying. "He reminded me that we are not supposed to be doing any investigating and that it could be dangerous and mess up his investigation."

"Shhh." The person at the other table glares at me. I glance at Jacob, shrug, and then bend over my book.

Chapter 25 – Pastor Clark

A dusting of snow has covered our quaint little village. Starkly white against that backdrop, the houses are a sterile testament to the coming winter and Yankee Puritanism. The only relief from the starkness of the homes is the elegant trim and extravagant windows. The bare branches of spreading maples create a tunnel of grey lace under which I am walking. Ancient stone walls line the road, punctuated by drives and walkways into each front yard. The only breaks in the monotony of white clapboard are an occasional brick house and the handsome stone turret of the library.

It is the first winter without my childhood friend. She loved the first snowfall, when it was not quite cold enough to freeze over the ponds and streams. The white flakes dropping softly onto the ground contrasted with the black water of the ponds. If it was quiet enough you could hear the snowflakes fall 'like frozen dove's tears' she would say. She loved that the animals could still get around and would leave their footprints for her to follow and investigate. Those of opossum, raccoon and skunk were scattered about near the river, where little creatures were still to be found and eaten with gusto, leaving behind a shell here and a crawfish claw there. The fox and squirrel and mouse also leave footprints in their hunt for food, attempting to stash away a cache or gorge enough to put on some winter weight. A skirmish with a hawk is evidenced by the large fan-patterned wing-feather prints in the snow as well as deeper impressions of the battle and small drops of blood. To Diana it was a world full of movement, excitement, life. Winter teemed with animals busy trying to survive.

She showed me so many things about the natural world around us. She had a reverence for all things and didn't hold herself above even the smallest creature or plant. This first snow again reminded me she was gone, and I knew the arrival of each new season would bring further realization of how much I had lost.

She had a strong conviction that all things alive had a season, and once it was over they would eventually all return to their original form as part of the earth. She didn't think that was bad. It was the natural cycle and we should, she thought, embrace it all. We should rejoice at not only the part when we emerge and grow and thrive, but also the part when we decline and finally go back to our universal mother. She thought that if we could accept with understanding our inevitable demise and change of form, we could find peace and purpose in these years we are allotted to walk the earth. She thought it sad that people felt the need to seek the reason, the purpose for life. To her it was simple. We are animals and our mothers bore us, and that is the reason we are here.

She was wise beyond her years, but not everyone agreed with her. She didn't usually share her philosophy. She said she had had enough battles with people over it, so generally she kept it to herself. But she shared it with me. She also sometimes had discussions with Pastor Clark, who at first disliked her visits, telling her they were a waste of his time. He would get angry with her, believing she didn't respect his age, wisdom and senior standing as a clergyman. What did a silly teenager know about life and higher philosophical thinking? Religious faith, he said, was what families and communities and morality were based upon. Believing in and worshiping a supreme being were tantamount to our purpose in life. We would be nothing without God. But Diana argued with him and he would end up shooing her out so he could get done what he said was *real work*. As heated as these arguments would become, Diana said she liked the pastor and she thought he liked her. She felt he enjoyed these little visits. He would always wave when he passed her on the street, or stop to speak with her if he had time. Twice he went to the Turners' house for dinner. It was his custom to visit his parishioners for dinner and he would try to get to every family at least once a year. He admitted to Diana he would visit a family several times a year if the dinner and wine were especially good. Diana invited him to her house twice. With her mother's help she would try to put on a nice spread and socialize with the pastor, but her father and brother would wolf down their food and disappear. They left Diana and Anna in embarrassed silence until Pastor Clark brought up the subject of Diana's menagerie—Cecil, Harry, the three mousers—and the conversation, re-started, became lively. But he visited only twice. He told Diana he didn't have the time, but she knew there was another reason and it was likely her family's uncomfortable aura. It wasn't enough that her father and brother were not willing or able to be sociable and showed him such disrespect, but here was the daughter who fought his teachings at every level. Her mother Anna was not a strong believer either and could take or leave the church. When she did attend she said it was because she didn't like the feeling of being judged by the villagers, who believed that at least one family member had to be a regular churchgoer. So to keep the peace she would show up once a month. This was a family lost to Pastor Clark and they all knew it.

Yet Diana liked him and often dropped into his office in the back of the rectory. She would stand at the door, looking in the window. If he was there alone, she would knock softly and he'd look up from his work, smile and wave her in. She might bring up the last sermon or ask what the sermon would be the next week, and they would talk about it. Sometimes his wife, whom Diana also liked, would come in and offer them tea.

Diana thought one of the reasons he liked her was that she saw him as a man and not just The Pastor. At times she said she would talk to him about how poorly people treated her and how little she liked most of them. He usually listened and said nothing, but once in a while he would remind her that she put herself on the outside. She went out of here way to be different but then didn't like it when people shunned her. She could see his point. But she said she just wanted to be accepted as she was. She didn't want people to try to bend her to fit the mold they wanted her in. He said he could understand that.

All this is what I am thinking the next day on the way home from school. I decide to visit the pastor, with whom I have never had the kind of relationship Diana did.

I go up the driveway to the rectory and peek in the window. Pastor Clark is alone, and I knock gently on the door. He jumps, sees me, then rises and lets me in. "You surprised me," he says without rancor.

"Sorry. I didn't mean to. I just remember Diana told me how she would come to visit you at your office." His back is to me as he returns to his desk.

"Come on in and sit down." He gestures open-handedly at the chair across the desk from him and sits down after I do. He looks fatigued. "I miss her. She was such a bright and lively girl. She was a breath of fresh air." Frowning, he pushes his glasses up onto his forehead and tiredly rubs his eyes with the palms of his hand. "Excuse me. I haven't thought about her for a while." He pulls his glasses back down but his eyes are rimmed red.

"So what brings you here today?" He turns over some of the papers on his desk and tidies them into a neat pile while he talks.

"Do you really think her death was an accident?" He makes me nervous and I can't bring myself to make small talk.

128

He stops mid-shuffle and looks hard at me.

"Do you?" he asks, apparently unsure how to answer the question.

"No, I don't think it was an accident. She was just too sure-footed in the woods, by the river, on the rocks. I find it hard to believe it was an accident." I pause, hoping he will fill in the silence.

"I'm not sure either," he finally says, shaking his head. "But the constable ruled it an accident."

"But the constable says it is still an open case. I talked to him recently."

"Really?" He looks to the side, cocking his head thoughtfully. "If it wasn't an accident, what could have happened?" Thoughts of the possibilities are washing into his consciousness, raising his eyebrows higher and higher.

"Jacob and I have been talking about it. We just don't think she would have jumped or fallen in accidentally. We think something precipitated it, maybe not someone actually pushing her, but maybe someone making her so upset that she didn't care and didn't know what she was doing anymore." Pastor Clark stops and shuffles his papers again. "We think she was acting strangely the last month or so before it happened. She just wasn't herself. We don't know why. Do you?" I haven't planned to ask that much, but there it is, right out there.

"I agree. She wasn't herself that last month. She would stop in and argue and be so out of character. I once felt she was mocking me when she started discussions, but that last month she seemed in earnest, much more argumentative, very angry. I didn't know what to make of it at the time. I thought it might be her home life, and I asked her, but instead of talking about it she only seemed to get angrier. It was odd. I thought it might just be some kind of teenager thing because I had no idea why she was riled. And then she was gone." He looks down at his hands that are folded on his desk. "Did I not do enough? I don't know. I don't know," he says, shaking his head.

"Did she say anything else? Did she talk about anyone she didn't normally talk about? Do you have any clues?" He sits looking at his desk for maybe a minute.

"No, I can't think of anyone. Why don't you speak to her doctor? I don't think she was feeling well, but it wasn't any obvious ailment. Talk to Dr. Hunt. He may be able to help you."

I thank him and leave, feeling much better now that I have another person who might be of assistance. I walk home through the snow, slipping on the slick sidewalk.

That night I open Diana's diary again.

Chapter 26 – Seventh Entry – The Runaway

Diana Turner
May 5th, 1937

I HATE my father. Hate him. When I told him about Mr. Anders offering to help me with college, he forbade it, absolutely forbade it. I am so distraught. My hope for an education, for a future, has been thrown away. Why, I asked him, WHY? But his response was as though I were a child: "Because I said so." I have come up to my room to write. I have my door latched and I am insanely angry. How could anyone be so ignorant? I scream into my pillow, and then cry into it. How unfair. Harry comes over to try to comfort me and I kick him away. Oh dear, what is the matter with me? Harry is my dear sweet protector, just trying to comfort me. I'm sorry, Harry. He forgives me and licks my hand. I don't know why my father is against it. I can hear them downstairs, my mother trying to talk reasonably to him and my father yelling and swearing. It may have to do with pride—maybe he thinks if he can't take care of our household no one should. But he's been only marginally caring for us. My mother said that since he had the accident he will never rise up in the company but will be kept in the same position, barely scraping by and getting only the minimum of raises. My mother must stoop to working for other women in the village so that, as she says, we don't "end up in the poor house." I'm even getting a job soon in the mill so that I can help.

My mother said he was once a handsome and proud man and that the accident made him bitter. But he needn't spread his bitterness into my world. He should let me fly. Maybe he doesn't want his daughter doing better than his special son. I cannot imagine what he's thinking. I just wish he'd die.

Diana Turner
May 9th, 1937

I thought I might have some luck with my father after Mr. Anders came to visit.

I told Mr. Anders that my father was against it and he said he would visit and try to talk to him. Mr. Anders is a reasonable man.

I was there when my mother let Mr. Anders in. My father was engrossed in a radio program and was angry at the interruption. He dismissed every point that Mr. Anders made: Diana could earn her own living; she wouldn't need much more tuition if she could get a grant and with his help he was sure she could get one; she could get out of the town and move up in the world. With each point my father grew angrier and angrier, until finally he told Mr. Anders to leave and not come back. "And DON'T think you're going to seduce my daughter!" At that Mr. Anders blanched, finally looking angry, and shot back, "If you weren't Diana's father I'd think you hated her." He turned and walked up the street. My mother stood in the door looking after him and then glared angrily at my father. He just looked disgusted and sat down in his easy chair to go back to his radio program.

I was of course crushed. I screamed at him, then went to my room and cried and cried. When my tears were exhausted, I banged down the stairs, Harry following, and out the back door, slamming it after me. I walked and walked and walked, up the river and on paths I'd never been on before. I couldn't go back—I was too angry, too hurt and upset. I wanted to run away but I hadn't brought anything with me. How would I stay warm? How would I feed Harry?

Finally it was getting dark. I didn't know where I was but I knew I was not too far from the river and that I could follow it back down, but I couldn't do that now. I would get hurt trying to walk in the dark. I had on a heavy wool shirt so I wasn't cold. I looked for a place we could curl up together and found a stand of hemlocks, dark and dense. The hemlock needles made a cushioning as soft as my mattress. I moved a few sticks out of the way and huddled under several trees that grew close together and Harry lay next to me as near as he could get. I was exhausted, and soon fell into a sleep that was broken by a barred owl hooting close above me. After that I couldn't get back to sleep, but dozed on and off for a while. By the time it was getting light I was starting to get so cold that even Harry's long body couldn't keep me warm.

I followed the river back down to the house. I vowed to myself not to speak to my father unless it is absolutely necessary, which is basically never. My mother looked relieved and came to my room with poached eggs and toast and asked me where I'd been, telling me she'd been worried. She said Jeffrey went out looking for me but came home as it got dark and said he couldn't find me. No one called the constable. I could have been out there dead in the river and they wouldn't have cared. That's not true—my mother would have cared and Mr. Anders would have cared. Pastor Clark would have cared. Jacob and Hanna would have cared. Harry and Cecil would certainly have cared.

I hope that I can make enough money at the mill to get a room somewhere. Maybe someone in the village has a spare room they can rent me. If I make enough money I won't have to go back to school. I will be away from here anyway. I want nothing more than to be out of this house where I am not valued. I feel sorry for my mother; she is trapped in this stultifying family. The monotony must have sucked from her any ambition to be something other than a drudge.

Diana Turner
May 12th, 1937

> *My father is finally noticing that I am not talking to him. He wears a forlorn face, but occasionally I catch a sideways glance that seems almost lecherous. All I want to do is come home and go to my room to avoid all his creepy looks. I have taken to bringing my supper upstairs and eating in my room using the excuse that I feel ill. I don't want to spend any time with him at all. My poor mother asks me to come down and eat with them but I cannot. The thought really does make me sick. When will I be able to escape?*

Chapter 27 - Dr. Hunt

I knew that Diana was having a hard time at home, but I had no idea to what extent.

Now I have to worry about whether her father influenced her in any way. It is impossible to imagine a father driving a child to her death. That would be a sad, sad story. Given my sweet although imperfect family, I cannot feel anything but a great sorrow for her and her family, a family that must have been more impacted by her death than a family on good terms, or at least that is my rationale. So many problems and ill feelings unresolved. How can you resolve problems once a person has died? How do you make amends? How do you say you're sorry? How many times have each of them gone back and imagined doing things differently? Would Mr. Turner have been less rigid if he had known the outcome?

I've decided to take the pastor's advice and visit Dr. Hunt's office, which is in his home in the village, just a few houses down from the library. When I stop in on the way home from school today, the office door is closed and a sign hung on it says he is with a patient. In the small alcove that serves as a waiting room I hang my coat on the coat rack and sit in one of the two chairs. I can hear muffled voices coming from his office and finally after ten minutes his patient emerges, closes the door, puts on his coat and hat and leaves. Dr. Hunt comes to the door to see if anyone is in the waiting room. "Hello? Hanna Smith? Is that little Hanna Smith? Goodness, you have grown. You don't have an appointment. Do you need to see me?" I say yes as I enter his office, which is also his exam and treatment room. I have not been here in years. My body responds viscerally, remembering how scary it was to have to get a shot. But today I relax, knowing I am not in the office for a shot or for any medical purpose at all.

"Please sit down." He motions me to the chair in front of the desk as he takes the seat behind it. I am able to quickly scan the large room, which is airy and brightly lit from the windows on its north side. A tall white scale stands in one corner but the rest of the examining equipment is behind a curtained screen in a large alcove. In another corner a woodstove flanked by a waist-high brick partition gives off comforting warmth. A large glass jar of lollipops sits on his desk and the brightly colored treats within invite children to forget their fears. I take in things I'd never noticed before. A large ornately framed diploma graces the wall next to a framed magazine cover featuring a doctor preparing a shot for a young boy who is looking nervously at the doctor's diploma.

"What can I do for you today, Hanna?" Dr. Hunt jolts me back to my purpose.

"Hi. I haven't been here in ages. I guess I'm healthy." The doctor gives me a quizzical look, tipping his head down to peer at me over his spectacles. "I'm not really here because I'm sick or to have you check a problem. I'm here about a friend of mine." I take a deep breath and launch in.

"You were Diana Turner's doctor, right?" A look of understanding now replaces the quizzical one as he nods. "I was her best friend, and I am still curious about what happened. You see, I don't think she committed suicide and I don't think she slipped and drowned either. I think something happened, something really bad. I knew her pretty well and I think it's suspicious. So I'm wondering if you had seen her in that last month or two before it happened, before she drowned. I'm wondering if there was a problem. Was she sick? Could you even tell me if you knew?"

Dr. Hunt gazes first at me and then down at his hands. His elbows rest on the arm of his chair, his fingers spread as he taps his splayed hands together rhythmically. Then he presses his palms together.

"You know we take an oath to practice ethically and we are also compelled to keep confidential our patients' information." My hopes fade at those words. "And there is also, as you probably know, an investigation still ongoing regarding her death." I nod. "However, I know you were her friend, and she *is* dead. So I understand this is more than just curiosity for you." I nod again. "If I speak to you, can I trust you to keep our conversation confidential?"

"Yes, absolutely, but can I share it with Jacob if I don't tell him where it came from?" He looks at me seriously, his eyebrows going up. "That's no longer confidential, is it?" I am confounded; I cannot tell Jacob that I got this information. "Okay, I won't tell him. I promise." He continues to study me in silence. "I promise," I say in a firmer tone.

"Can I ask why this is so important to you?" He wants to know what brought me not only to this conclusion but also to the point where I find it necessary to follow up on it.

"She was my friend. I thought her death very odd. Now, as time goes by, I'm finding things that I never expected, things she didn't tell me. So I want to find out from people who knew her if there were other things I didn't know, other things that were going on that she didn't talk about, things that might have influenced her. Do you understand?"

He nods. "Okay, but you must swear that anything I tell you is kept secret, and know that if for some reason it gets out, I will deny I ever told you. I hope you don't make me regret telling you. Maybe you will find some peace when you finally find out one way or the other what happened." I look at him expectantly and he continues. "Diana was not often sick. I would see her when I went to the school for the simple exams the school required. She was fit as a horse, healthy, strong and smart. I find it odd that the poorest families often seem to spawn the healthiest offspring. Anyway, a few months before she died she came in to see me complaining of headaches. I examined her and noticed bruises on her upper arm, strange ones that looked like someone had tried to restrain her. When I asked her about them she made up an answer about getting caught on a branch when she was out walking. She was nervous and I didn't feel she was being honest. She quickly changed the subject. I didn't think she was having migraines but I gave her a low dose migraine medicine just to see if it would work. It didn't and she came back the next week. She seemed upset, agitated, but I could find no reason for the headaches. I was concerned that something was wrong at home, but when I asked her about it she just shrugged it off, saying there were no problems at home, none at all. I tried another medication, a stronger one with a mild narcotic." He looks down at his hands. "I never saw her again. I sent several letters to the house asking her to come in, but she didn't. Then about four weeks later she was dead. I really felt as though I should have done more, but I didn't. So there you have it. I tried, but I failed her." The doctor rises, walks over to the window and looks out. "As a doctor you lose patients. It's natural. People get diseases, they get old or they're careless with their health. But you never expect to lose a perfectly healthy young person. That is hard to accept, and it's hard on the parents. I've seen marriages break up over the death of a child. It's a sad day..."

"Thank you, Doctor. I'm sure you did everything within your power."

When I go to sleep that night, I have the drowning dream that I haven't had for a while and awake in terror gasping for air.

Chapter 28 – Ghost?

I have a lot to think about after seeing the pastor and the doctor. Having to keep some information to myself is difficult. I want to tell Jacob what the doctor told me but I can't.

I meet Jacob at the library after school. I spill out my stories about the diary entry where her father was so against her going to college and about her running away for the night and then about my visit with Pastor Clark.

Jacob listens but seems impatient, and when I finally get to a point where I can pause I ask him what is going on.

"My parents are on the warpath again. They think my grades are slipping and that I need to get a lot more studying done so I can get them high enough to get into college. They're blaming it on you. They're saying that instead of studying I'm just goofing off. I can't get them to see that I am trying but that I'm just slower than their golden boy." He gives me a guilty look.

"Don't worry." I try to let him know it's okay. "I can help you with some of your classes. You'll do fine."

"No, no. I've been told I can't meet you anymore. This is our last study time together." He looks angry and dejected. "Now I know how Diana felt, like she was always at her father's mercy, that she couldn't make choices for herself. She felt 'trapped like a wild animal,' she said." I can see his frustration. He is holding his pencil so tightly that it snaps. He puts his head in his hands and I can see he is crying. Now I too feel helpless.

"Listen, don't feel bad. It will all work out. You can probably get some help at school. Talk to the vice principal. They can get you a tutor, I'm sure."

He lifts his head from his hands, looking at me with red eyes. "But I won't see *you* anymore." His voice is pained. "When will I get to see you? Only in those quick moments when we pass in the hall."

I am taken aback. What is he saying? I like him, but haven't to this point thought of him in any other way than as co-conspirator in our quest to find out more about Diana. I don't know how to respond.

"Well, we can work on this on our own. I can pass you a note when I find out something really interesting." I am trying to comfort him.

Jacob reaches across and puts his hand over mine. His tone turns pleading. "Don't you see? I've grown to care for you. I *need* to see you." This is scaring me. He's never acted like this before, and from what I can tell he hasn't been attracted to me. He has never mentioned anything except that one time when he said that to throw people off we could pretend to be dating.

"I thought we were meeting about Diana, to find clues as to what happened to her, right?" I am trying to be rational, to be sensible.

"Well, that was how it started out, but I've grown fond of you. Haven't you grown fond of me? Once I thought you had. Was I kidding myself?"

"Jacob, of course I like you. You are a good friend, and it is gratifying that you're interested in helping me work on this. I'm very happy that you agree that something odd happened with Diana and that we can work together. But your parents want you to work on your studies. Don't you think that's a good idea?" I watch him as he sits up straighter and wipes his face. He looks at me coldly.

"You don't feel the same way. I can tell. Do you even like me at all?"

For a second I think he is pulling himself together. Then he looks angry, and then seems pathetic.

"Please, please don't leave me. I need to see you."

"Jacob, I don't feel the same way. I just don't."

"But," he says hopefully, "it could change. You might like me more at some point, right? You can't rule that out, can you?"

I am troubled by his insistence. "Listen, I wanted to do this with you. I wanted to search for clues about Diana. For me it was always about Diana. I'm sorry if you misconstrued any of my actions, but I don't think I ever led you on. And for now I think you need to follow your parents' advice and spend more time studying."

"You act so self-righteous, but you're not that good of a person. I know what you did. I know you broke into the Turners' house. So don't act like you are so superior."

Now I just want to escape. I feel this is dangerous territory. He is privy to so much of what I've seen and done lately, and he may use it to manipulate me. I feel doomed. I've never seen him like this. He is irrational. Had Diana seen this side of him? I think of going home and telling my parents everything, and hoping they will forgive me, discipline me, and keep me home, safe from the outside world.

"You don't mean what you're saying. We are friends allied in a common cause. I never meant to lead you on. I didn't lead you on. What is going on? Why are you acting like this?"

He puts his head in his hands again. "I don't know, I don't know." He sniffles. "I feel awful. I can't sleep anymore. I can't concentrate. I think I'm coming down with something." He looks up at me. "I'm sorry. I don't know what's come over me lately."

The librarian walks in to shelve a few books. We both bend over our schoolwork, looking studious. After she leaves

Jacob appears more composed. "My parents are right. I need to focus more on my studies. I have been slipping." I watch as he presses his palms to his temples and grimaces.

"Do you feel okay? You don't look well."

"I've been getting bad headaches. They come and go. Some days I feel okay and others I don't feel well at all, and I can't figure out why." He lowers his hands and then reaches across the table but I withdraw my hand.

"I have to tell you something. I'm afraid you will think I am insane." I shake my head no and he goes on. "The other night I thought I saw Diana. I thought I saw her walking up the road in a white dress. The dress was shimmering like it was moving in a breeze. I watched her and thought, It's cold out and she should have a coat on. She looked up at me in the window. I waved, but she just stood there, and finally she turned and walked away. It was a beautiful shimmering moonlit vision. I don't know if it was really her. It made me want to follow her, but when I went downstairs and out to the road she was gone. It was very still. Cold and still. I loved her and I still miss her. It would have been just like her to be out walking on a moonlit night." I am relieved that he has moved past needing to see me and I hope he won't go back to it.

I offer a tentative question. "Do you think it was a ghost? Do you think it was *Diana's* ghost?" His eyes are on his book but I can see he is looking past it, gazing at a vision. "I don't know, I don't know," he whispers, shaking his head. "But I want it to come back."

"I realize we have to get home soon, but I'll see you at school. We can have lunch together, okay?" He looks up and nods. "See, we won't be totally disconnected. I can tell you more about what I find and you can tell me too. We can still work on this." I am trying to be positive, reassuring, without implying anything else. It is a fine line I am stretching out to him, trying to give him some encouragement but not too much. It is so out of character for him that I have to think he is getting sick and maybe not getting enough sleep.

That evening I have a restless night myself, tossing, turning, and finally, once again opening Diana's diary.

Chapter 29 - Eighth Entry - A Job

Diana Turner
May 20th, 1937

School will be out soon and I will be working. It is only this thought that keeps me from trying to really run away. Jacob has been very understanding about this and says that once he graduates from college he will come back and marry me. He says we don't even have to live in this town anymore. I know that even if that did happen it wouldn't be for years to come. But just that he offers it to me, offers to marry me someday, makes my existence more bearable. Someone finds value in me.

I am so unhappy with my life. The only joy I get is from my animals and my walks. School now seems pointless. I had never dreamed of college, but once Mr. Anders gave me the hope of going it was all I could think about. Now I no longer care. Would it matter if I got A's and B's or D's and F's? Who would care? My father thinks that only my foxy brother has any worth and he instills in his son the same sly morality that he has nourished in himself over the years. His worth to the mill after his accident had been reduced to less than a regular worker. They kept him on but he was dismissed as broken, not valuable, and that ate at him. He became bitter and would find little ways to cheat the company. He would bring home the ends of paper rolls and use them to wrap fish entrails or give them to us kids to draw on. The company looked the other way. His thefts were of little consequence and the bosses, when they did notice, felt bad for him and thought they owed him at least the loyalty to keep him on since he had been injured at their mill. He hated them, and the thought that they pitied him made him hate them more. One of his little acts of contempt nearly burned the mill down. He left a lit cigarette butt outside the door and the smoldering leaves and debris started a small fire, which fortunately was seen and doused before it became larger. He is teaching his son to be as disrespectful of the company as he is. But Jeffrey knew when to be sly and when to 'butter them up,' as he said; that way he always stayed on the boss's good side. Jeffrey never trusted anyone at the mill. He pretended to have friends, but my father instilled a deep mistrust of people who were not family and Jeffrey never let them in on any of the shenanigans he might be up to. Even though they were small infractions, he kept them between his father and himself. I think he does them only to please my father. So I am, as always, an outsider. And now even more so since I am friends with the boss's son. At times they ridicule me at the supper table, but now I barely ever eat supper with them.

It will be interesting when I start working there. I would be tempted to turn both of them in, but then everyone would turn on me, I'm sure. There is always the mentality of the workers that they stick together, even if it is with people they don't like for things they don't agree with. For if they ever broke ranks the other workers would make it unbearable to work there. It is always the workers against the management, or at least that is how it seems to me. I will need to be very careful. But if I can stay out of trouble and away from the guys I know are trouble-makers I should be okay and able to save up some money. I can hardly wait.

Diana Turner
July 18th, 1937

Finally I am working. I just got my first pay envelope and have dumped it onto my bed and Harry and I are counting it over and over. I am thrilled. I am spending some of it on animal food. I promised them all treats once I got working and the butcher has said that when I can give him a couple dollars he can get me a big bone and some real meats for Harry and the cats. The bone is free. It's the other that will cost me a little, but not much for the amount he is giving me. Harry dances with me, his paws on my shoulders, and when I sing he makes funny little noises. After a minute my mother hollers up to keep it down, that my father will be home soon, and Harry and I go back to counting the money on the bed.

I saw a beautiful dress last month. A white one, of such thin soft cotton that it seemed like silk. I'm going to buy that with part of my salary and then I'll save all the rest. Whoopee, Harry, we're rich!

Chapter 30 – Wraith

Now it has happened to me! I am more frightened than I have ever been in my life. Last night after reading the diary and falling into a deep sleep, I was startled awake by the faint sound of someone calling me. It sounded like a woman's voice and just outside, but when I rose and went to the window I did not see anyone. The pale and waning moonlight shone on the lawn and threw skeletal shadows of the bare maples onto the snow. Then a movement caught my eye and a flash of white moved swiftly along the road. It looked like a woman in a dress and it disappeared into the trees along the road. I nearly fainted. Leaning on the window sill I strained my eyes in the dim light trying to catch a glimpse of it, hoping for and dreading its return. I was shaking and chilled to the bone. I did not know if I should go outside and try to find it or if it was indeed a wraith and impossible to conjure unless it wanted to be seen. I stood there for many minutes but finally, cold and exhausted, I climbed back into bed. I was still shaking and I didn't know if it was from cold or from fear. I was thankful that my sisters were usually heavy sleepers and didn't hear it. Or did I hear it? Did I even see it? Was it a figment of my exhausted imagination? I lay awake for a long time, shaking, thinking about what Jacob had said. He *did* see something. He did see Diana. I thought he was just overwrought and under pressure from his parents, feeling ill, suffering from insomnia. It was easy to explain away his vision. Now I feel guilty for doubting him. This is becoming more and more frightening. Was it truly Diana's ghost coming back to lead us to a murderer? Or is it Diana telling us to let her spirit rest?

What should I do? I decide I will try what Diana would have tried if she were me. I will attempt to contact her spirit. Tonight I will bring a candle late to bed, wait for my sisters to fall asleep, and then take out her special possessions—the Tarot cards, the dagger, the rock and her diary—and I will ask her what she wants. If she hears me I know she will tell me what I should do.

I don't know what to do about Jacob. Should I tell him that it's happened to me or should I just keep it to myself? Given that he was so distraught the last time we met, it might be best to keep it a secret for now, and if I can reach Diana I will tell him then.

My sisters are asleep and I have a candle lit on the table by the window. I have spread out the Tarot cards and put the dagger and the crystal upon them. What should I do next? I look at this collection of hers. It seems potent and powerful. I know this will work. I try whispering her name: "Diana, Diana, Diana, are you here?" I chant it slowly, quietly. I am calling her. "Diana, can you hear me?" Then I repeat it all, whispering slowly. I wait. The flame flickers and then goes out. I can hear my name again from the lawn: "Hanna. Hanna. Hanna."

I can see from the window the white figure moving swiftly out to the road.

I think it's a person.

I rush to put on my robe and shoes and I speed down the stairs as fast as I can without falling.

Moonlight still washes the snow and I can see footprints on the lawn where the wraith was. I run out to the road, only to see the white figure disappear around the bend. I could never catch up to it. I don't even try. Examining the footprints I think they look large for a woman, certainly larger and heavier than

Diana's ghost would leave. I put my foot into the impression. It is about two inches longer than my footprint.

As I go back upstairs I think about the whole encounter. Who? Why? I am still shaking a little, but this time I think it is from excitement. I put away Diana's possessions. "Diana," I whisper to myself, "I will find out what is going on." I tuck the box of her things under my bed. My mind keeps running the short scene over and over. The voice and the vision—who was it and why?

This whole day I have been thinking about it. We went to church this morning and from the back pew I could survey the congregation. Since it is just before Christmas the church was filling up more than on other Sundays. I looked at the people as they came in. The Turners were not in attendance, and the Sparkses do not go to this church, but Dr. Ross was there with his wife, and Mr. Anders with his wife, and Constable Cruthers with his wife. All of them gave me a small sign of recognition, either a smile, a small wave, or a nod. When Pastor Clark came in he smiled at me. His homily was about families, friendship and our relationship to God.

About halfway through the service Jeffrey came in, panting and red-faced, as though he had just run all the way from his house. He sat in a back pew and glanced around as though searching for someone. Once he saw me he stopped, clasped his hands in prayer and bowed his head. He did not look at me again and left immediately after the service ended.

When we filed out Pastor Clark was on the steps to greet us. He took my hand and said he was glad to see me and hoped all was well. My mother and sisters looked at me as though I were a stranger. What is going on that I am personally recognized by the pastor and called by name? Dr. Ross came over also, shook my hand and said hello. Mr. Anders nodded to me and Constable

Cruthers tipped the hat he had just put on as he left. My mother regarded me oddly. I knew this was going to be a topic of conversation when we got home.

As I predicted, my mother asks why I am "so popular," but I minimize it, saying I have been visiting with the pastor on occasion and that I saw the doctor at the market. She is too busy fixing a big Sunday dinner with us to question me any further and I hope I've satisfied her. Later at dinner she brings up how popular I am, but Grace, figuring I've been snooping around, says it is good to have a person in the family so well–connected, and after a couple minutes the conversation turns to our school classes and our plans for spring planting.

In bed tonight I open the diary hoping to find a few more clues to the identities of the note-writer and the person trying to frighten us by dressing as a ghost.

Chapter 31 - Ninth Entry

Diana Turner
August 22nd, 1937

I am still working but this is not the dream of independence I was hoping for. It has turned into drudge work equal to what my mother does but without the respect of anyone, either my employer or the other workers around me, who seem to hate having a woman in the mill.

My father, at the few suppers I attend, rails angrily against the mill, the mill bosses and the unfairness that he believes has befallen him. My brother looks on without interest. My mother focuses on her dinner, trying not to let my father's ongoing rancor over his position at the mill spoil her appetite. When the long painful meal is over my father retires to his armchair near the radio and lights the first of his constant string of cigarettes. My brother goes to his room with a new comic book. Even at twenty he's still reading silly junk. My mother and I clear the dishes and clean up. I slip outside to give Harry and Cecil some table scraps, which they gobble up quickly.

My father—what a self-centered twit. I have lost all respect for him. I work at the mill and am treated worse than even the youngest and most incompetent boy working there. They think because I am a woman I am less, but in my heart I don't go along with that. I know I am just as fast and almost as strong as some of them. I know I am competent, I know I am valuable. They will not break my spirit. They will not see me cry or whimper or complain, because I am a woman. I've come

151

to believe that women are stronger than men, not physically, but they can endure more. They can endure more abuse, more pain, more insults. We are in many ways superior. We have to prove ourselves, so therefore we have to do more and do it better.

They have broken my father's spirit. They killed it when they kept him on after the accident, giving him menial jobs. If they had fired him he would still have the pride to fight. Even with only one good arm he would have found something he could do to be useful, to feel needed. But they took that option away from him and he had a family to support and wasn't willing to look at other options. So he became a loafer, someone who smiles at the bosses but insults them behind their backs. He encourages others to find ways to cheat the company, as though the accident ruined not only his arm but also his moral code. I once felt sorry for him, but now I feel only contempt.

My mother, who once was beautiful, is now just a drudge. She is caught in a miserable life because she has no future outside of this mean marriage. Like my father, the family, the children, are what keep her in bounds. The family narrows her choices but she's not as bitter as he, though she is downtrodden. Her attempt to make a slightly better life is at the expense of her pride when she works for the women in the village who have the means to pay for her help. She is poor and pathetic, but still I love and respect her more than I do my father, who does not want to see me rise above my entitled brother. It is ludicrous because my brother won't ever do anything with his life. He will always be a line worker in a mill because he has no initiative, no drive to be better. I hate my life.

What do I have ahead of me? Work at a mill where everyone shuns me? Will I be able to save enough money to be on my own? Not unless I could share with several other girls. I certainly would not be able to afford it otherwise, and if I did do it I'm sure the town would create a ruckus. Sharing living quarters with other girls is unheard of in a small town like this. We would be considered immoral, as if living in a house of ill repute. If I were in the city I might be able to. But would it be so hard to become established there. So the only chances I have to escape would be to work as a domestic in one of the local homes or to marry someone. Marry someone.

Jacob has said he would marry me once he graduated from college. I know that is beyond reality. I know that Jacob will find another girl when he goes to college or his parents would create so much pressure that he would be unwilling to go against them. So I would likely be marrying a local boy. But whom? No one else has been interested in me, only Jacob. I think they are afraid of me. I find it hard to be like the other girls. They have nice clothes and act silly around the boys. The boys like that silliness. I am not able to fake the little giggle or the coy looks. Why can't any of them see me and like me for who I am? Why is it that the only boy who can see and appreciate me is one who will probably break my heart?

What am I going to do? My senior year is coming up this fall and I have no plans. Will I be a miserable millworker like my father or a sad drudge like my mother?

My brother is a worthless sleazy nitwit and I always try to avoid him.

Pastor Clark says this is just a phase I'm going through, that in a year or two my life will seem much better and not to worry about it so much. A year or two still seems like an eternity, and what am I to do in the meantime? But Pastor Clark is one bright spot. He likes to talk with me and will sometimes sit for an hour of conversation about philosophy and what books we're reading. I had just read a

153

Hermann Hesse book called Demian *and we talked at length about that. Sometimes his wife comes in with tea and little biscuits and we have a nice visit. I feel special at those times. Those are the bright spots in my life.*

Mr. Anders also is a bright spot. He loves to talk about our classes, and sometimes I talk about my home life and he tries to console me. But it's not as much fun with him anymore, not since I've been denied a future.

Of course Jacob is a bright spot, but that too is tarnished because I know the reality of the long-term prospects. I really care for him, but there is no future. Even so, there are times when I see his tall frame in the distance and it brings my desire for him to the surface like a fire on water. I cannot let him know how I feel. He is too innocent and would be shocked.

Why do I seem to do best with older married men? Are they less threatening? Do they really appreciate my intellect or do they just feel sorry for a bright girl trapped in a dull family? Or are there desires smoldering in them as there are in me? Hush, hush, my insistent hormones.

How will I ever get out of this endless cycle?

Chapter 32 – The Tarot Cards

I wonder if the ghost has appeared at Jacob's home again. I want to talk to about it. At first I was relieved to know it was not a ghost but now I am frightened that there is a person privy to our scheming, someone who knows we're looking for something. That person probably wants us to stop looking, and maybe wants to scare us. I can think of only one person who would want to do that: Jeffrey.

I am going to try to find out if he is the ghost, although I am pretty sure he is. Why would he want to scare us? I guess the answer to that is pretty simple. He's guilty, or feels guilty. But we can't just start accusing him unless we're sure.

The problem I see now is that Jacob and I are not supposed to be seeing each other or talking. I will pass him another note and see where we can go from there. Otherwise I will have to do this alone. Although Grace was a willing partner I doubt she would want to immerse herself in this as much as I have.

The note I have written:

Hi. I have seen the ghost too. It came by my window Sunday night. It is a person. I want to find out more. I think it is J. We probably should not be seen together, even at school. If you want to work with me we should use notes, but destroy them once we've read them. I am going to try to find out more about J. Destroy this note.

I slip it to Jacob at school on Monday when no one is around. He tries to talk to me but I tell him we can't. Maybe I will get a note back.

After school I go directly home, not stopping at the library. When I get a chance to talk to Grace I find she is willing to hear about my adventures but doesn't want to involve herself and says she will deny everything if our parents find out. I think that is fair. I tell her about the ghost that is not a ghost. She thinks it is crazy anyone would go to such lengths to frighten two school kids. But I explain that we might be getting close to the truth and that someone is getting nervous about it. She understands. I tell her if it happens again I will wake her but she will have to be careful not to wake Ida, who would reveal the whole thing to our parents.

I cannot figure out how to expose Jeffrey without either catching him or breaking into the Turners' again. The thought of entering that house another time gives me the creeps. Maybe we can trick him into exposing himself as we did Gilbert junior. Maybe we can somehow get him to implicate himself. But how?

I've got it! We turn the tables on him. I have some of Diana's most prized possessions. I will plant them where he will see them and then watch his reaction. I will be the ghost this time.

Some of the winter snows have already come and gone, as has Christmas. Christmas had only the amount of fanfare a farmer's family could manage with chores still to be done, animals still to be fed and tended to. The only changes to our regular routine were an extra visit to church, a large dinner, and an exchange of gifts on Christmas Eve.

It has been one of those winters without much snow and a warm spell has made it totally disappear. This is to my advantage. I choose a spot carefully. On the trail that runs from

the mill to the Turners' is a dense stand of hemlocks. It is so dark
and dense that if you are only a little into it no one can see you. I
conceal myself carefully in it, far enough from the path not to be
seen but close enough to see the one spot on the trail where I will
leave my sign, one of Diana's Tarot cards. I have chosen the
death card and on it I have written in handwriting that I think is
as close to Diana's as possible: "Why, Jeffrey?"

I know that Mr. Turner will come by first and I will need
to be quick to leave the card after he's gone and before Jeffrey
comes through. I wait, and soon Mr. Turner comes up the path,
one arm dangling uselessly and the other putting a cigarette to his
mouth that he draws on, coughing as he continues out of sight.
When I am sure he can't hear me I quickly slip out and place the
card in the middle of the path face down. I want to see Jeffrey's
reaction when he finds it and turns it over. I slip back into the
trees and wait. It seems like forever and soon it will be dusk and
hard to see. Finally I hear him coming. He's whistling.

When he's directly in my line of sight he looks down and
stops. I see him bend down and pick up the card and turn it over.
He blanches. His eyes get big. He looks to be in shock. I hold my
breath, afraid to make a sound. He stares at the card for a few
seconds, then recovers and looks around as if to see if anyone is
there, if anyone is watching. He gingerly puts the card into the
breast pocket of his jacket. It's almost as though he doesn't want
to touch it. He looks behind him down the path towards the mill.
Finally he starts walking slowly up the hill. He's no longer
whistling.

It was satisfying to see Jeffrey afraid. If he was the ghost
he has gotten a dose of his own meanness. He looked frightened
and guilty. But is it proof? Not enough. Do I chance doing it
again? I want to, just to be spiteful. I go home and try to pick
another card. Which one would be equally threatening and

ominous? The Magician, the Fool, Justice, the Hanged Man, Judgment, the High Priestess? Which one? I settle on the High Priestess. If I can, I will do it one final time with a third card.

I go to the trail the next day. On the High Priestess card I have written: "Jeffrey, you have wronged me. D."

I conceal myself as before and slip out to place the card as I did the one yesterday, then go around to the back and nestle myself into the small spot in the hemlock grove that shelters me so securely.

Jeffrey comes up the path much as he did the previous day. He stops and looks down at the card. He seems afraid to pick it up. He looks around, scrutinizing the area thoroughly. I am grateful I chose my hiding place so carefully. He looks into the dark hemlock grove but cannot see me in the deep shadows. He finally picks up the card, turns it over to read it and immediately drops it. Standing there for several moments he finally bends over and picks it up, looking closely at it now. Then again he puts it into his pocket.

"Who are you? I know you are not Diana. Why are you doing this to me?" Jeffrey's voice is strong, sounding bold, but there is an underlying tone of fear barely discernible. He looks around once again before continuing on his way.

I cannot help myself. I must do this once more. I choose the Judgment card and go back the next day.

As before, I go to the back of the hemlock stand, entering from above. Each time I use a slightly different route, trying not to make it obvious there is an entry point, .trying not to break branches or muss the leaves on the ground. The elder Turner pauses in front of the trees to pull out a cigarette and then a metal lighter. I hold my breath, waiting as he lights the cigarette and then goes on walking. I dart out to place the card in the same spot and quickly return to my hiding spot.

Jeffrey comes along slowly this time, looking carefully in all directions before he picks up the card. He reads the words: "I will be avenged. D." He looks angry and this time tears the card in half and throws it into the bushes. He screams, "I AM INNOCENT!" I probably start but he doesn't look my way. He tromps up the path with deliberate, pounding steps.

After he's passed and is out of sight and earshot I let out my breath.

Oh dear, am I wrong? *Is* he innocent?

That night I again awake gasping from a dream of drowning. I lay terrified, cold and sweaty.

Chapter 33 - The River

These harrowing dreams are haunting me. I am compelled to go down to the river, to the pool. I've given Jacob a note explaining that I need to go, asking him if he can escape unnoticed to meet me there on Saturday afternoon so I can explain to him the outcome of my latest exploits.

Talking to Jacob usually calms me. Most of the time he is so level-headed. I want to share everything with him. I hope he can meet me.

In the next two days, waiting for Saturday, I think about all that has transpired, all the information we've uncovered. We're fairly sure that Diana's death was not an accident, and that she would not have willingly drowned herself. This conclusion is our justification for our search for a responsible party, for who might have actually pushed her to her death or who would have driven her to such madness that she felt compelled to suicide. As caring friends we cannot accept any other reality.

Saturday arrives, and after getting my chores done and packing a sandwich I head towards the village in hopes of meeting Jacob by the river. I walk past the Turners' and over the bridge that leads to the pool. Although it is a sunny day I am bundled up; the winter chill still holds us in its snowless grip.

The well-worn route is sun-dappled, the leafless trees allowing light to filter through to the layer of dead leaves I walk upon. Jacob waits at the entrance to the path leading to the overlooking ledge from which the boys like to jump. Normally we would enter from below the ledge, a vantage point showcasing the low waterfall as it drops into the pool.

I cautiously pick my way over bare roots and large rocks until suddenly we emerge on the ledge. I am uneasy. This once peaceful and welcoming spot is now shadowed with an uncomfortable pall. Why did we come here? I'm beginning to think this was a bad idea. Jacob walks unsteadily onto the rocks. He seems unusually nervous. I begin to have misgivings. Can Jacob be trusted? He seemed to have a burst of irrational behavior the last time I saw him. Coming here may have been a very bad idea. I am unsteady too. The rock ledge has icy spots I need to be careful of. Jacob senses my unease and steps back to take my elbow and guide me. But I cannot move. I feel paralyzed.

We are almost overlooking the pool. As he creeps closer to the edge, I am consumed with dread. I am horrified. I scream and move to pull out of his grasp. He is startled by my scream and almost loses his balance.

"What are you doing?" he asks sternly. "You almost knocked me in." I pull away from him and slip.

That is the last thing I remember until I awake with Jeffrey hovering over me gently slapping my face.

"Hanna, are you all right? What happened?"

"I remember." It is all I can say. "I remember." Jeffrey looks at me, puzzled. "What's going on? Why did Jacob leave you here?"

Now I am very confused. "Why are *you* here and where is Jacob?"

"I was out with Harry in the woods and I heard you scream. When I got down near here Jacob was running out in the other direction yelling, 'Watch out! Watch out!' I yelled to him asking where you were and he paused to point back at the pool and I found you here. I don't know where he went. What's going on?"

"We were looking for clues to the accident." I hesitated, not knowing how to phrase it. "We were looking for clues and Jacob panicked and I fell."

"Are you okay?"

"I think so, but something happened." Jeffrey watches me as I sit up. "Something happened. I remembered what happened that day. Oh, my God, I remember."

"What do you mean you remember? You found her, right? Wasn't that what happened?"

"Yes, but I was there with her when she fell." I am feeling as surprised as he is. "I was there."

Jeffrey looks at me incredulously. "What happened?"

He takes my hand and pulls me up and I sit upon a nearby boulder. "Now I remember it all. I had been looking for Diana and I found her here by the river. She was very upset about something. She was ranting about the job, about Mr. Sparks, about school, about her father. She was hard to follow because she was angry about so much and ranting on and on. Different topics ran into each other and made no sense. Then she complained of feeling ill and pressed her hands to her head and screamed. The way she was acting frightened me. We had been walking down here and she veered away from the lower path and went towards the upper one where the ledge is. I was worried because she was so irrational. I followed her up. She was very agitated. I'd never seen her like that. And then it seemed as though she was going to jump into the water. I went to grab her and got hold of her arm, but she pushed me away and I fell off the side. I must have been knocked out because when I awoke I was on the rocks right there." I point to where I fell. "I don't know how long I was unconscious. I was freezing and my legs were in the water. When I looked around I saw Diana. She was mostly underwater, caught on a rock. I ran around the edge of the pool and pulled her out. But she was dead. There was a gash on her forehead, but no blood. She was cold and blue and not breathing. That's when I ran back to your house."

Jeffrey listens intently, nodding his head now and then. "So," he says, "it was an accident?"

"Yes, but she was acting very oddly, out of character. She wasn't herself."

"You thought it was me, didn't you?" I nod. "That was you on the path, wasn't it?" I nod again.

"Do you still believe I had anything to do with it?"

I shake my head. "But you misbehaved with me. That was wrong."

He looks carefully at me. "Yes, I did. I thought you liked me. I thought you were interested in me. I don't know how to act. I've never had a girlfriend." He seems honestly contrite. "I'm sorry."

"Diana said you misbehaved with her too."

"Not really." He shrugs at this. "That was when we were younger. You know how kids roughhouse. It might have gotten improper a few times, but I think we outgrew that. She remembered it though, and was cautious to steer clear. I just wanted to have a sibling to talk to, but she wouldn't even accept that. And she hated that my father so obviously favored me. I don't blame her for that. I think a lot of the bad blood between us was caused by our father."

"But you read her diary, didn't you?"

"Yes." He looks down at the ground. "I was worried about her. I didn't trust the Sparks boy."

"I wonder what happened with him. Where did he go?" I say, finally getting back to the present.

"I don't know but he sure went out of here fast."

"I can't go to his house. His parents don't want him to see me. I'm not sure what to do."

"He's a big boy." Jeffrey is reassuring. "I'm sure he found his way home."

Jeffrey helps me up and points me toward the path. "Wait. I have to get my lunch." I am unsteady, but I manage to climb the path to the top of the ledge where I dropped my sandwich when I fell. Jeffrey follows me.

When I get to the top I look out once more at the pool. I don't have the feeling of dread I had when Jacob and I first climbed up. I have an unusual sense of calm, of knowing what had happened. The sun comes out and warms the ledge.

"Do you want to share my lunch?" I decide to eat here if I don't have to eat alone. He nods and sits on the ledge as I unwrap the sandwich and open the thermos of tea. Handing him half the sandwich, I look out at the river. The waterfall roars and I have to talk loudly to be heard above it. "It's beautiful here. I can understand why Diana enjoyed walking these paths." He nods and bites into the sandwich.

"Do you feel like you have the mystery solved?"

"Well," I answer, "some of it."

"What? There's more?"

"I'm not sure. Diana wasn't acting right. She wasn't herself. I want to know why. Do you have any idea?" I look at him, hoping for a sign that he knew, but he just shrugs. "I don't know. She wasn't talking much to me."

"I want to find out what was going on. Tell me. If you knew, would you tell me?"

He looks hard at me. "What do you think?" He asks this with a half smile.

"I don't know."

"I would tell you. But other than the ongoing anger with my father and her reticence with me, I don't know what was going on. She was certainly weird the last few weeks or month before, but that's all I know. She was angrier, more volatile. She

164

said she felt sick and spent more time in her bedroom than she typically did. I'd hear her up there banging around. I don't know what she was doing. If you think I did something, you're wrong."

"You may not have done anything, but something happened." Jeffrey nods.

We walk back to the road and at the Turners' Jeffrey stops, and asks, "If you find anything out will you tell me?"

"Yes, I will." I head home, wondering what has happened to Jacob and knowing I can't go to his house to find out. He just left me there. What if I were really injured? I am troubled by his reaction to my falling. He was acting almost as strangely as Diana.

I want to read more of the diary but know I won't have time until tomorrow.

Chapter 34 - Tenth Entry - A Clue

The next day at church I look around and in the back corner sits Jeffrey. When I catch his eye he smiles. That evening when I get into bed I open Diana's diary to the next entry.

Diana Turner
September 1st, 1937

I am happy that I have the job. As much as I hate it, the extra spending money really helps. Harry is looking a little heavier and I can't feel his backbone anymore. Cecil is dancing on the branches now.

The supervisor at the mill has it in for me. I'm sure it is at Mr. Sparks's behest. I'm cleaning toilets and the men seem to have gotten messier. What hatefulness. But I do get to spend time with one of the technicians, who is teaching me some of his work and skills. He likes me and that helps me to feel I have some value. He thinks women can do the same work as men and he wants to help me. He's doing it on the sly. Anyone who found out they would probably report him and I bet he would be demoted. But he's smart and it's making the miserable job much more tolerable.

School has started and I'm trying to juggle my studies with the millwork. It will be a challenge, but so far I'm managing. They are letting me work four hours in the evenings and that's when I'm getting trained. Working part time I can still get enough cash to keep my animals in feed. I have a new animal. I found a raccoon that was injured and I'm keeping it in a cage in the back of our shed. I have to keep it a secret, but so far no one has noticed. I'm calling him Bandit. He looks like he was injured by an automobile. I've been bringing him hard-boiled eggs and bread and some milk when I can get it. He gobbled down the eggs and when I went to put fresh water in his cage he bit me, but it's just a scratch. He is a cute little devil but is not as fond of water to wash his food in as I've heard raccoons are. I have to fight to keep Harry away from him. I found some boards and made a makeshift fence out beyond the cage to keep Harry away. Seeing Harry sends Bandit into a fearful state and he cowers in the back of the cage.

I hope that Cecil finds a mate next spring. He should be raising a family. Sometimes I hear crows nearby and I watch him. He turns his head and listens and seems interested and sometimes even cries back, but so far he's still living the good life with me. He is so smart. I don't know what I'd do without him and Harry. If he does mate I hope he stays close and visits often, and maybe brings his family by.

Jacob still walks home from school with me but since I have to go to work we cannot tarry long. Sometimes now, when we're out of sight of the village, we walk hand in hand. I know he's afraid of his parents. They barely tolerate him just walking me home. If it ever became more they might pull him out and put him in a private school. They have threatened to do that. He says his brother treats him worse than a leper and relentlessly badgers him about me. Why should this matter to them? Am I such a big threat? I would think I would be inconsequential to them. Maybe that's part of the problem. With his father being a supervisor, and most of my family being poor mill-workers, the Sparkses are embarrassed that their son is smitten with a low-class girl. It must be hard to worry about who you can socialize with and who you can't and be constrained by that convention. They're probably thinking I am trying to snare a rich boy, son of the supervisor, that I'm plotting and scheming to reel him in like a trophy trout. If they only knew how Jacob fawns on me and how I am the shy one. I don't think he is deliberately trying to shame his parents by seeing me. But I have on occasion wondered if he was doing so without realizing it. Honestly we are not seeing each other or even dating, not in my mind at least. We are friends, but he would like it to be more. If I were one of the village fancy girls, I'd consider it. I would be more on his level. It would be a realistic liaison. But I know that as much as I too would like it to be more, it is truly impossible. There is no real future. I probably should break off even the friendship. It will have to happen at some point and I will be hurt and he will be too, but not as much as if we were to get more involved. And I sometimes want to get more involved. I want to release my repressed inhibitions, to let go. Why should I be so cautious? Why don't I just throw myself into this as I would if I really were the gold-digger the Sparkses think I am? But what if I got pregnant? What then? I still would not become his wife. I would be the shunned girl, the foolish, careless girl. Sparks would likely pay my parents off or they might even deny the parentage and force Jacob to deny it too.

I cannot. All I have is my honor. I have nothing else. I am not rich. I have a poor future ahead. What can I offer anyone but my honor? My mother says it is a tragedy that someone as smart and kind and good as I am is trapped in such pathetic circumstances. But I know in my heart that I am above so many others. I know I outshine the dimwitted girls who giggle their way up and down the halls of our school. I know I have more power and more abilities than any of them. I may not be able to buy a fancy dress to wear to a dance or a camelhair coat, but I could survive in the woods for days without anything but my wits and my knife. How many of them could say that? They are all ninnies. I am their superior. But I will never be able to marry Jacob and any one of them probably could. I am sometimes embarrassed by my table manners, which seem inferior to theirs. But I was not raised to hold my little finger up or not to slurp from my soup spoon. How unfair life sometimes seems.

Diana Turner
September 14th, 1937

I am very sad today. Little Bandit has died. I could not save him. I buried him out behind the shed inside the fence I built to keep Harry out. I put a pile of large rocks over his grave so I don't have to worry that an animal will dig him up. He was rigid when I found him. I covered him with a towel that I stole from the house. I put a hardboiled egg in with him for his journey and found some asters and goldenrod that were still blooming and I put them on the rocks. Harry sat with me as I said a few words, but then I had to put him outside the fence or he would have tried to dig up Bandit. The poor little thing. I hate to see animals suffer. Why must things suffer? Why can't we just have clean, painless, fearless deaths?

Sometimes I think I shouldn't try to save the injured animals. I think that I do little good and maybe harm. Nature will take care of those that are well enough to survive and it will let succumb those that are too weak to live, whose death intervention would only prolong.

I have to say that I have on several occasions just tried to ease an animal's fear and agony as it dies. An injured baby rabbit that the cat caught I put into a cardboard box with grass and just covered it with a towel. I knew it would die soon and I left it in a dark, comfortable and quiet spot so that it could die in peace and not be tormented by the cat in its last minutes. I

guess I am learning how to let go of these creatures, but it is
hard. I'll miss little Bandit.

That is the last entry in Diana's diary, the last entry. There is no
clear clue as to what happened from then on.

Chapter 35 - The Constable

I am anxious to see Jacob and be sure he is okay. It was so out-of-character for him to run off on me like that, although he has been acting strangely lately. I would like to think he was frightened and going for help. I do think I would have wakened and been okay, but it was nice that Jeffrey came and stayed with me. It made me feel better. I have gone from feeling unsafe around Jeffrey to feeling at least relatively comfortable with him. What was it all about when he attacked me in Diana's bedroom? Did he really think I liked him and believed it was okay or was something I wanted? If so, it was very poor judgment on his part. I will reserve my judgment and let some time pass before I decide if he is trustworthy or not.

Jacob was not in school yesterday. I have become very worried about him. The walk to school this morning was quiet, and as classmates joined me on the sidewalk I couldn't help but hesitate and look up at the Sparks house. Large and white, it commands respect. The curtains were closed and it looked as though no one were home. Jacob did not descend the granite steps and join us as he did almost every other day. Someone turned to me and said, "He must be out again today." And I nodded. People know we are friends and don't seem very surprised at my looking up at the closed door.

I have decided to visit the constable today after school to tell him my revelation of the previous weekend. If Dr. Hunt's office is still open after that I will stop in there too. I want to know what happened. I want to know why I didn't remember being with Diana until I revisited the river and the spot where the event unfolded.

After school lets out I walk to the town hall, picking my way around muddy leaves. The winter seems to be coming to an end and an early spring is evident in the swollen tree buds and the sap from broken maple twigs dripping onto the sidewalk. Upon seeing me enter, the constable closes the file he had open, rises, and taking his pencil and pad directs me to our spot in the library.

"Hello, Hanna, how are you?" I say I am well and that I have more information that might be of interest to him. When I tell him about Jacob's parents he nods and says they have been in to see him.

"Yes, they came to see if I could do anything to discourage the 'farmer's daughter' from getting their son into trouble. I told them that unless someone was committing a crime I couldn't do anything and who their children dated was their responsibility, not mine. That did not sit well with them, but I reminded them that our office had already turned a blind eye to some of their indiscretions. You can imagine that brought our discussion to an uncomfortable close."

"You said that to them?" I am incredulous.

"Yes, and you should remember that our discussions are confidential."

"Yes, of course."

I go on to tell him about the ghosts that are visiting both Jacob and me. Then I relate my story of returning to the river ledge for the first time, my revelations there, Jacob's running away and my talking to Jeffrey. Constable Cruthers listens closely until I finish and then questions me.

"Jacob accompanied you to the ledges against his parents' wishes?"

"Yes. I've been having nightmares about drowning, I had to go back there," I explain.

"And when you went out on the ledge, you remembered?"

I nod. "Yes. Something happened. I fainted or something and it all came back to me." The constable waits for me to go on. "I think that when I was out there with Diana I fell and hit my head, but I didn't remember it until last Saturday." He continues to watch me carefully until I become uncomfortable.

"You don't believe me, do you?" His gaze does not waver. "I swear I didn't remember until Saturday. I went down there because I thought it might help get rid of the frightening dreams I've been having. It was shocking to me to remember. I had forgotten that I'd fallen. I just remembered seeing her in the water and pulling her out."

"Do you remember anything else, anything at all?" I shake my head.

"What about these ghosts you're seeing?" He seems cooler, less open, as though he's become a different person.

"Well, Jacob told me about a ghost at his house, and it really frightened him. He awoke and when he looked out he could see it walking in the moonlight. Then it disappeared. He was convinced that it was Diana's ghost. He was frightened but also wanted to see it again. Then it happened to me, the next night. I was asleep and I could hear a woman's voice calling my name. When I got up and went to the window I could see the ghost. It walked along the road and disappeared. The next night I set up a shrine to try to contact it and it came back. When I went downstairs to get closer, it ran away and I could see footprints in the snow where it had been. So then I knew it wasn't a ghost but a person who was probably trying to frighten us. I suspected Jeffrey, but after talking to him on Saturday I don't think it was him. Now I don't know who it could have been."

The constable is listening but looks distractedly out the window. "You're sure it was a person? What did it look like?"

"I didn't get a good look. Both times it moved quickly. It looked like a woman. It had on a long white dress, but the footprints in the snow were big, a couple inches longer than mine."

All the while we are talking he is writing on his pad. One line on the pad says "The River" and there are lines indented after that. The next line I can make out is "Ghost" and more lines are under that. I am reading upside down so I can't make out the other writing.

"Is there anything else you remember about the ghost?" I shake my head again. I guess I am not that good a sleuth. I can't remember any important details.

"Has anything else been happening?" He looks at me, putting his pencil down. I decide to tell him about the Tarot cards on the path.

When he hears what I did with Jeffrey and the cards he shakes his head.

"You know," he starts out sternly, "you are taking too many risks in this business." He looks at me as seriously as he did the first time I saw him. "What if Jeffrey was involved? What if he saw you and tried to hurt you? What would you have done? Do you want us to find your body down at the pool too?"

He writes "Tarot Cards" on his notepad.

"I thought I was safe. I had planned it out very carefully."

"Don't you think," he continues in his serious tone, "that Jeffrey knows every inch of those woods and probably knew someone was in that hemlock grove?" I have no answer.

"What else? Do you have anything else to tell me?" Constable Cruthers is starting to sound exasperated.

"Well, I have her diary. I read it all and have it with me. You can have it." I pull the diary out of my pile of books.

The constable slams his hand down on the desk and makes me jump.

"That's it! That's the last straw. That is withholding evidence. You could be in big trouble for that!"

"Yes, sir." I look down, close to tears.

"When did you get this?" he asks a little more calmly.

"I'm not sure, maybe six weeks ago. Jeffrey let me into her room."

"You were in Diana's room with Jeffrey? Was anyone else in the house?"

"No." I don't meet his eyes.

"You...." He is speechless. "I should tell your parents what you've been up to. You are going to get hurt. I'm really worried about you. You are not using common sense."

"I know, but I was being careful. I thought I could take care of myself."

"You're a girl and no matter how smart or strong you are, if someone wants to harm you, they will." I nod and look down at my hand that I scraped when I fell at the ledge on Saturday.

"I won't get involved anymore," I say apologetically.

"Now, do you have *anything* else to tell me?" I shake my head.

The constable gets up, gathering his pad and pencil. "Now go home and stay out of trouble. If I find out anything I'll drop by your house and tell you."

I am heading out the door. "Okay."

Chapter 36 - The Ghost

I am grateful that the constable didn't decide to see my parents. He is right. I might have been in dangerous situations. I always felt in control but I trust people far too much. Somehow I can't imagine people trying to hurt other people or wanting to do them harm. I especially can't imagine anyone wanting to do me harm. But I suppose that if a person is threatened, he might do what is necessary to protect himself.

When Tuesday goes by with no sign of Jacob I become afraid he is in some kind of danger.

After school on Tuesday I stop by Dr. Hunt's. He waves me in and I tell him the whole story of what happened the previous Saturday, about losing consciousness on the ledge and having all the memories come back to me from the day Diana died. He listens solemnly and nods as I explain it all to him.

"Yes, yes, I've heard of this. It's a type of amnesia brought on by a traumatic event and often it is reversed when something triggers it, like a reliving of the event or a return to where it occurred. This does happen. So, you were there before she drowned, but didn't see anything after you fell?"

"Yes, I was there. I told the constable all about it. And I didn't see what happened after I fell. She may have hit her head or someone could have come along and pushed her in. I don't know, but she was acting strangely, very agitated and upset. I don't know how long I was unconscious and I'm sure she was dead when I pulled her out."

"Well, I thought she may have fallen accidentally. All this lends more evidence towards that outcome. You didn't see or hear anyone else by the pool before or after you lost consciousness?" I shake my head.

"Okay then. I'll add this to my notes." He writes some notes on a sheet of paper.

"How do you feel now? Do you feel dizzy or have fainting spells other than those you just described?"

"No. I'm usually healthy as an ox."

"Well, if you remember anything else be sure to tell Constable Cruthers and me." He turned to open a drawer and pull out a file.

"Okay. Bye." I put on my coat and go out through the empty waiting room.

Wednesday I look again as I pass the Sparks house on the way to school, but still no Jacob. After lunch I am just settling into my homeroom classroom when I happen to look out the window that faces the road and I see someone in a white dress streaking down the road towards the school. I can't believe my eyes. I watch as it comes closer and closer, wildly waving something in its hand.

It is Jacob, heading towards the entrance to the school. I get up and ask to be excused and I dash to the entrance to meet him.

He comes running down the hall shouting, "It's Gilbert! It's Gilbert! I found this dress in his closet!" He is flushed and panting. Doors into the hall start to open and several teachers come out. Before they can approach he rushes to me. "Look! I found this note too!" He holds out some papers and I take them.

"Are you okay, Jacob?" I am worried because he is acting so irrationally.

"Yes, I'm okay. Isn't it great I found them!" He is wildly throwing his arms about as the teachers come to see what the commotion is about.

In this strange white dress thrown over his shirt and pants, thrashing his arms about, he looks almost insane.

"Jacob? Jacob? Are you all right?" One of the teachers comes closer.

"I'm fine! I told you, I'm fine!" He turns towards the voice as a second teacher comes from the other direction and takes hold of his arm.

Jacob turns to see who has his arm and tries to pull it away as the first teacher grabs his other arm and more teachers rush into the hall to assist.

"I'm fine! What are you doing? Leave me alone!" Struggling to free himself he not only flails his arms but also starts kicking at the teachers restraining him. Suddenly all three fall to the floor and other teachers help hold Jacob down while the two on the floor retain their grip on him. There are now five teachers trying to maintain their hold as Jacob thrashes about screaming for them to let him go.

One of the teachers tells another to go to Dr. Hunt's and bring him to the school and get Constable Cruthers too.

Soon kids are pouring into the hall and crowding around in a circle three and four deep. More teachers arrive and start trying to disperse the group.

"Come on now, go back to your classrooms. There is nothing to see here. Go back to your rooms."

I watch as they roll Jacob over onto his stomach and continue to hold him on the floor. The students begin to leave as Dr. Hunt and a teacher run down the hall. The doctor elbows his way through the remainder of the crowd.

"Please let me in," he says, his tone calm and assured. Once he is close to Jacob he kneels and opens his bag. "Jacob? Jacob, are you okay? What's going on?"

Jacob has stopped struggling. "I had to show Hanna. I had to show her what I found."

Dr. Hunt continues to talk gently to him. "If we roll you over, will you be calm? I want to check you out and make sure you didn't hurt yourself when you fell just now." Jacob grunts yes and the doctor motions to the teachers to turn him over.

He is flushed and looks frightened. The doctor opens his bag and takes out a thermometer.

"You don't look good, Jacob. Can I take your temperature?" He nods and Dr. Hunt puts the thermometer into his mouth, still talking calmly. "I know you can't say anything right now, but you have something to show to Hanna?" Jacob nods and both of them look at me as I put the pieces of paper behind my back and look intently at the two of them. Dr. Hunt asks, "Did you stay home from school today?" Jacob nods again. "Were you ill? Is that why you stayed home?" Jacob nods and then shakes his head and tries to speak. "Just a moment and I'll take that thermometer out and you'll be able to talk." In a second Dr. Hunt's eyebrows go up as he looks at the thermometer. "You are sick. You have a very high temperature." He puts the thermometer back into his bag. "Do you think you can walk? I want you to come right over to my office." Jacob nods. The teachers help him up and with one at each elbow start to walk him to the exit, the doctor following. As they approach the door the constable arrives, and Dr. Hunt says, "We have a very sick boy here. Will you accompany us to my office?" And they all leave.

Back in my classroom I watch them walk Jacob down the sidewalk towards the doctor's office. Only then do I look at the papers Jacob handed me.

Chapter 37 – The Note

Sitting in the classroom I feel my teacher and classmates watching me. I try to look calm as I put the papers Jacob gave me into my school book. I open a second book and try to read. The class goes back to their studying.

I am very flustered and anxious to see what the papers hold but I know I cannot do anything that will arouse suspicion.

I cannot wait for school to let out but the day feels like the longest one I ever remember.

When school is finally over I go first to Dr. Hunt's office. It is closed and a note on the door says he has gone to the hospital and will not open the office until tomorrow. I take this as a very bad sign.

I want to look at the papers before going to see Constable Cruthers so I head to the library. I sit at our favorite table in the turret of the library and I'm grateful that no one else is here.

I unfold the papers. There are three of them, all on the mill's letterhead. They all contain various threatening messages, including "Tell him he had better leave you alone or I will KILL HIM!" I stare at these papers spread out in front of me, all in the same handwriting as the original note I found in Diana's book. I can hardly breathe I am so excited and frightened. I want to see the constable and wonder if he is in his office. I fold up the papers and head for the town hall.

Constable Cruthers has left for the day, says the last person still there. He is straightening papers and rattling keys so I know he is anxious to leave.

I go home.

Still agitated by the afternoon's events, I try to do my chores quickly. When Grace arrives and we are setting the table for supper I whisper that I want to talk to her later and she says we can do the dishes together.

Supper cannot come and go quickly enough for me. I am so excited to be able to tell someone about the day. Finally we are at the sink and making enough noise to ensure that no one else can hear us.

"Did you hear anything at school today?" My voice is just above a whisper.

"Yes. I would have liked to talk about it at supper but I thought this was what you were going to bring up and that maybe you didn't want anyone else to know."

"Thank you," I whisper gratefully. "Jacob went crazy."

"Yes, I heard. I'm surprised Ida didn't say anything about it."

I tell her about the phantom that was not a phantom and how I found the footprints in the snow and how I went with Jacob down to the river and fainted and remembered being there before Diana fell in.

She stops me now and then, asking questions and wondering aloud why I hadn't told her when these things were happening.

"I'm not sure. I guess I was afraid you'd tell Mom and Dad and I would be forbidden to go out at all and I needed to find out what happened."

"Well, what else did you find out?"

I continue my story: how my suspicion that Jeffrey was the ghost led to planting the Tarot cards, how he found me by the river after Jacob ran off, how I am pretty sure now that he wasn't the ghost, how I am still baffled by who could have caused Diana's death.

Grace asks about my being there with Diana before she died and I tell her I fell and thought I hit my head and that Dr. Hunt said that sometimes people forget things until something jogs their memory and then they remember.

Then I tell her about Jacob running into the school and yelling that he found the dress, the ghost's dress, in Gilbert's closet, and that he handed me papers he'd also found there.

"I've got the papers upstairs. I'll show them to you." She says she is eager to see them, and as soon as all the dishes are dried and put away we go upstairs, telling everyone we need to study.

I pull the papers out and show them to Grace. "What do you think? They are on the mill's stationery." I am leading her to the same conclusion I have come to.

Grace agrees. "I think Gilbert senior wrote these. Who else would use this letterhead? I think he was practicing making his handwriting look like a younger person's, and he was trying to decide what would be most effective in frightening Diana away."

"I agree. He probably knew that an outright threat would only make Diana angry and less likely to back off. I think they were desperate to protect their son from someone they imagined was a gold-digger." Grace nods in agreement. "I think they also put Gilbert junior up to playing the ghost to try to throw us off the trail, to scare us into dropping our search." I am drawing conclusions as I talk. "I'll bet that if I hadn't seen his footprints and realized it was a person and not a ghost that the ghostly visits would have escalated with threats to scare us into stopping our nosing around."

"I'll bet you're right."

"I hope that Jacob is all right. When I went to Dr. Hunt's after school it was closed and you know he's almost never closed."

182

Grace gives me a concerned look. "We'll find out tomorrow."

"I hope so."

Chapter 38 – Jacob

When I get to school the next day my teacher calls me to his desk.

"I've been asked to send you over to Dr. Hunt's office. You can leave now and come back as soon as you can."

"What is this about?" I want an answer but the teacher tells me to just go directly over there.

When I arrive there are several people in the small waiting room so I stand. When the doctor opens his door to let his patient out he sees me and asks me to come in. I hang my coat on the rack and go in and sit on the chair opposite his desk.

Dr. Hunt looks hard at me. "How are you feeling?"

"I'm fine," I answer innocently.

"No headaches, sweats, weakness?" I shake my head. "Sit over on that table." He points towards the examination table. I do as he says while he gets something from a drawer.

"Open your mouth and let me take your temperature." I obey and he inserts the thermometer.

"Have you had trouble sleeping?" I shrug. I have trouble, I think, but mostly because of those scary dreams. "Have you been eating regularly? Do you have trouble swallowing?" I shake my head no.

He pulls the thermometer out, looks at it and relaxes a little. "So tell me about your sleeping." I tell him about the dreams about drowning that scare me. He watches me intently.

"Have you had any, ah, contact with Jacob? Have you kissed him?"

"What?" I'm shocked. "No! Absolutely not! We are just friends working together to find out what happened to Diana! We are just friends, no more!" I am emphatic. He continues to watch me carefully.

"Do you think that Jacob and Diana were more than friends?"

"Well, I know they really cared for each other. It's sad. I know Diana had no grand design upon him, and she even thought they might have to break off their friendship because his parents were so against it. I doubt they were more than friends."

"Do you think it's possible that they had, ah, anything romantic going on? Do you think they kissed?"

"I don't know. They may have kissed, but I doubt they did anything more than that."

"And you didn't have any kind of romantic attachment with Jacob? You're sure?"

"Yes, I'm positive."

"You said you thought he has been acting strangely lately. Tell me about it."

I described his odd actions at the library a few weeks ago, how strange he was at the river, and then yesterday.

"What's happened to him? What's happened to Jacob?"

The doctor hesitates. "I'm not supposed to be talking about this with anyone, but you were close to him. We think that he has rabies."

I sit back in the chair, sucking in my breath, overcome. "Oh! Really? Rabies?" He nods.

I sit there, looking dumfounded I'm sure, while all the implications of this diagnosis run through my mind.

"That's fatal, isn't it?" I am shocked.

He looks serious and sad. "It is fatal if it's not caught in time. We have a series of serum shots that can be used if we find out within the first week. After that there is nothing we can do except make the patient comfortable."

I realize why he's asking me about my relationship with Jacob and about his relationship with Diana. "Do you think Diana had it too?"

"It would explain her odd behavior.

"Now, I want you to stay home for a couple of weeks. Don't even go back to school. I'll talk to your parents. While I don't think you've caught it we probably should, as a precaution, start you on the serum.

"I don't want you to have physical contact with anyone in your family or any animals. This is just for safety. You can sleep in your bedroom, but have everyone make sure that all your utensils are boiled. Frankly I don't think you have it but I want to take all the precautions. If you don't think you can follow this regimen for the next two weeks, I will have to put you in an isolation ward at the hospital."

"I can do it."

"Your mother will be by soon to walk you home."

He goes to a drawer and pulls out a syringe and a bottle and draws the serum into the syringe.

"Lie down on the table and pull up your blouse." I do and he gives me an injection so painful that I muffle a scream.

"I'm afraid I will have to give you several more of these. I'll come to your house tomorrow morning and give you the next one, okay?"

I sit up and nod, tucking my blouse back in and rubbing my stomach.

"Don't rub or scratch that. You're probably very lucky you weren't exposed."

"Does this mean that Jacob is going to die?" It is unbelievable to me.

"We are starting him on the serum, but the symptoms have already presented themselves so it is probably too late. It's serious. Few people survive.

"Why don't you wait here? I'll see if your mother has come." I sit there, feeling exhausted, feeling drained, feeling sad.

When he returns he's leading my mother. He has her sit down while he explains to her what he has just explained to me. He is careful to be optimistic and tells her that this is all just a required precaution.

We leave the office as the Turners are arriving. Mr. and Mrs. Turner look grave. Jeffrey gives me a little smile that no one else can see.

On the way home we pass Mr. and Mrs. Sparks going in the other direction, towards the doctor's. Whatever they would like to say to me they squelch since my mother is looking very stern. I wonder how much they know.

My mother sends me up to my room, saying she will bring me dinner as soon as she gets a chance. She tells me to get a glass of water for myself as I go, and says we will talk later. I am *not* looking forward to that.

I fall into a heavy sleep that is punctuated by odd dreams and I awake at dusk with a dry mouth and the sound of dishes being done in the kitchen.

When Grace comes up and peeks in she sees that my eyes are open. "You're awake. You've slept most of the day. We didn't want to wake you. I'll go down and get you something to eat. Are you hungry?"

"Yes, but not too much; I'm not that hungry." I prop myself up and wait for my dinner, feeling as though I am not sick enough to get such royal treatment but remembering I have to stay away from everyone.

After a few minutes my mother brings me a tray. "So, you've been having quite an adventure," she starts in a scolding tone. "Eat this if you can." She puts the tray in front of me.

"Grace has been telling us about your escapades. We are very upset with you." My appetite wanes.

"I know. You should be upset with me. I know you told me to drop it and stay out of it, but things just kept happening. I'm sorry. I am so sorry."

"Now you've lost one friend and are about to lose another." My mother's tone is still scolding and she looks at me sternly.

I start to cry. The events of the last months have caught up with me and turned out to be more tragic than I could have imagined. "I'm sorry," I blubber.

My mother comes over and smooths my hair. "I'm just glad you're going to be all right. Thank God for that," she says, still stroking my head. "Now eat up if you can. You've got two weeks up here and you need to stay healthy." When she gets to the door she turns. "I'm sending Grace to the school to get your assignments and to the library for some books to keep you busy. You can get up and sit at the table if you want, but you can't come downstairs for a while. Your brothers and sisters will take up your chores for you, but you will owe them a lot of work to make up for it.

"Okay," I answer meekly. My mother smiles at me. "I love you, Hanna Banana." She knows I hate that name and love it at the same time. She turns to go and then turns back. "Oh, I forgot to tell you, not only will the doctor be here in the morning but the constable is coming by too."

She goes downstairs and I hear the dishes being done and a little quarrel going on between Grace and Ida as I eat my supper in solitude.

Chapter 39 – Solved

In the morning my mother brings up a tray of scrambled eggs and toast.

I am exhausted, and after nibbling a little I go back to sleep. I know Mom came in a few times to check on me, putting her hand on my head to see if I had a fever, and if I was awake she asked if I needed anything. She made sure I had water. I was being pampered. I knew that once I felt better and had more energy I would be disciplined. It was likely that for months I wouldn't be allowed to go to the cinema or out with friends for any reason. Even with all this coming to an unhappy end I am strangely at peace. I now know what happened. I don't need to be secretive any longer; my parents know or will know everything. It is a relief. Yet I cannot believe that Jacob is going to die. How could it have happened? How could he have become infected? The few moments when I thought he was a person I could care for were often short and fleeting. It might have been that I distrusted his family, that I couldn't imagine having a family so disagreeable that their values would poison everyone in it. But he did say his mother was different and he was close to her. I feel sorry for her and all of the Sparkses.

About an hour before noon my mother comes in to tell me to put on a robe because the constable will be visiting shortly. A few moments later she returns with a teapot and a tray of cookies and Constable Cruthers following her. She sets us up at the table under the window where my sisters and I do our homework.

The constable puts his hat on the table and sets down his pad and the diary I gave him a few days ago.

"Good morning, Hanna. How are you feeling today?"

"Tired," I answer, stifling a yawn.

"I'm not surprised at that." He actually smiles at me. "Well, it looks like your persistence cracked the case."

"Mine and Jacob's," I correct him.

"Yes, I guess Jacob had an important part in this." He pauses to put milk and sugar into his tea and take a sip.

"So, I said I would keep you up to date on what we find and I'm here to do that." He breaks a cookie in half, bites off a piece and takes another sip of tea.

"I know you are aware of the events at the school and afterward, but I'm going to go over everything so if my version doesn't sound like what happened you can correct me."

My mother taps at the door. "Do you mind if I sit in? My Hanna has been up to stuff we don't condone, and you can be sure she'll be disciplined for it, but we want to know the whole story."

Constable Cruthers looks from her to me. I shrug as if to say I'm fine with that. "Sure, Mrs. Smith, come on in." Mom pulls a chair up to the table. She has brought herself a teacup and fills it with tea and liberal doses of milk and sugar before sitting back and prompting the constable, "Go on. Don't mind me."

The constable repeats, "I'm going to go over the events from what we have pieced together. Hanna, if anything doesn't ring true, say something. I want to get this right." I nod and he begins the story.

"The Turners are a family of mill-workers. Ephraim and Jeffrey worked at the mill full-time, and Diana worked there last summer full-time and then started part-time in September when she went back to school. Anna, Diana's mother, worked part-time as a domestic in some of the village homes. They also had a small garden plot. Ephraim was handicapped after an accident at the mill but continued to work there in low-level jobs that he would never rise from. Jeffrey has been known to get into trouble now and again, but never anything serious. Diana was a very bright girl who excelled in biology but was never encouraged by her parents. She was not only quick and intelligent but willing to investigate and embrace ways of life that few people get involved in. You know what I'm referring to: some of the religions, including paganism, that she had studied and which caused some people to fear and shun her. She also had her mother's kind and generous heart and would take care of animals. She kept a stray dog, several cats and a crow and cared for other animals if they were injured." The constable pauses for a sip of tea and the last of the cookie.

"Mr. Anders thought Diana showed a lot of promise and wanted to help her get into college, but her father forbade it, alienating Diana and causing ill will between them." My mother looks over at me with her eyebrows raised. "She was doing that well? What a shame."

The constable continues. "The Sparks family was thought to be upper-class in relation to the other families in town. Gilbert Sparks, Senior was a supervisor at the mill and involved in town politics. It was rumored that he had extra-marital affairs. Gilbert junior was in college but still spending quite a bit of time at home. He was a clever student but always looking for the easy route to a goal. He had gotten into trouble with several girls and his parents paid his way out of those misadventures. Edmund was the quieter brother, without the winning ways of Gilbert junior or the desire to debauch the local ladies, yet he still seemed to have the values of the elder Sparks. Jacob, the youngest, was neither the scholar of the family nor in agreement with his father's values. He was close to his mother and took quite a lot of abuse because his father and brothers considered him a black-sheep. Marie, the wife and mother of the Sparks household, also suffered humiliation and abuse at their hands."

The constable pauses to pour himself more tea, adding milk and sugar, taking another cookie, sipping and nibbling. We too sip.

"Now we come to you, Hanna. You are from a good farm family. Grace and Ida, your older sisters, get good grades and will likely find good farming husbands and carry on their household skills. Hanna, you're a good student with many friends and you are considered level-headed. You don't discriminate against those from whom others might shy away; hence your friendship with Diana. You are a true and good friend, but it seems for the first time in your life you have let your good judgment lapse in the pursuit of solving this mystery."

He pauses for a sip. "How am I doing so far? Have I characterized the situation fairly well?" I nod, looking from him to my mother. "Yes, very well."

"Diana and Jacob had become friends, mostly due to Jacob's low-key pursuit of Diana. We don't really know why he found her so alluring. Maybe it was her ability to follow her interests without concern for other people's opinions. Whatever it was, it had his family riled up. The senior Sparks instilled in his two older sons, particularly Gilbert junior, the desire to break up this liaison, fearing not only a possible illegitimate child but also what they considered to be a girl seeking part of the Sparks inheritance. Am I correct?"

"Yes, I think that's correct." I nod and offer more tea around, which they accept.

"Here is where everything started to go wrong." The constable looks from my mother to me. "You read the diary; you know what happened. On September 1st of last year Diana found a sick raccoon, which she caged up behind a shed on their property. She put a fence out beyond the cage so her hound couldn't worry the creature. On September 14th the raccoon died of rabies. She didn't know the cause of death; she saw it had been

192

hit by a car and believed it died of its injuries. While she was caring for it, it bit her." The constable again looks at me with a very serious grimace.

"I didn't know. She didn't tell me. If she had I might have been able to help. I didn't get the diary until after she died, sometime in November." I am apologetic.

"I understand, but all this was an unnecessary tragedy, wasn't it?" I nod, rubbing my stomach at the injection site.

"Some of the rest of the story is obvious. Diana started to get sick and become less and less rational. While you were both at the pool she panicked. You fell and hit your head and were knocked unconscious. She fell, hit her head, slipped into the river and drowned. When you awoke you found her and went for help."

"Hanna." My mother didn't know about my I fall. "You didn't tell me you fell and hit your head. Are you okay?"

"Yes. I woke up cold and sore, but I was and am fine."

"Sometime between when Diana rescued the raccoon and when she fell in, she and Jacob had to kiss or have some other intimacy because Jacob now has rabies and is in very serious condition in the hospital." He again looked at us both.

"Hanna, at any time did he kiss you or have any kind of intimate contact with you? This is very important and you must answer honestly. Do you want me to ask your mother to leave before you answer?"

"No, no, she doesn't have to leave. We never did anything. We may have hugged once, but that was all. Nothing else. I'm positive."

The constable heaves a big sigh. "Good."

"Well, you saw some of the rest of the story. Jacob seemed to be losing his mind at school, ranting and wearing a dress that he said was Gilbert's. They brought him to the hospital, and he is in grave condition."

"I'm sure it was Gilbert's." I finish up what I know of the story. "Gilbert junior's, that is. When Jacob came in ranting I met him in the hall. He said he'd found it in Gilbert's closet, that Gilbert was the ghost who was trying to frighten us. Probably his father put him up to it. He also found these and gave them to me before the teachers came out and subdued him." I take the papers with the mill letterhead out from under my pillow.

Constable Cruthers scrutinizes them one by one, turning them over. He puts them on the table.

"When were you going to give these to me?" He is very stern. My mother too awaits my answer.

"I was going to give them to you the day before yesterday, but your office was closed when I got out of school. I guess you were dealing with Jacob. Then yesterday I was rushed off to the doctor's before I could get to you. I tried. I really did." I am feeling somewhat guilty but it wasn't totally my fault.

"I see." The constable examines the papers again. "I guess this solves the last bit of mystery of who wrote that note. I'm assuming that Gilbert senior was also trying to scare Diana away."

The three of us pause for another sip of tea, all of us eyeing the dramatic messages on the papers.

"Well." The constable picks up his hat. "Are you satisfied with your investigation? Do you think we solved the mystery?"

"Yes, I think we did."

Constable Cruthers rises, puts his hat on his head, and picks up his pad and the papers. "Mrs. Smith, thank you for the tea. Hanna," he smiles, "I hope I don't see you in my office again for a long time."

Before he goes out the door he stops and turns to us. "But if you want a job as an investigative assistant, I can try to get you into the college that will give you a head start in that field."

His glance goes from me to my mother, then back to me. "You would be a good assistant. I'd recommend you to the State Police."

He says goodbye and leaves.

Chapter 40 - The Turners

One Saturday during my quarantine the Turners come to see me. I am still in my room and my sister rushes up the stairs. "Quick, get some clothes on. You've got visitors." I hurry to change from my nightgown, which I'd been sporting for a week and was very tired of, into a simple, comfortable shift.

My mother leads the procession with a tray of tea and cookies and several cups. It looks like tea for an army. Behind her are Mr. and Mrs. Turner and Jeffrey.

I am somewhat embarrassed to have them in a room that is not very well aired out after I've spent a week in it. My mother, understanding my concern, opens the window. It is a warm sunny day, and in spite of a little chill the fresh air is welcome.

I throw a shawl over my shoulders and sit at the table as my mother and Grace fuss with setting up the teapot and cups and bringing more chairs.

Anna Turner speaks first. "I want to thank you all, all of the Smiths, for how kind you have been to our family these past years." My mother pshaws at her and gestures that it is nothing, then says, "We have a farm. What's a dozen eggs and a gallon of milk to us? We were happy to do it and happy to have Diana come and share our suppers with us."

At this Mrs. Turner wipes the corner of her eye with a handkerchief. "She always talked about this family. She thought the world of you. All of you, especially you, Hanna." Now it is my turn to wipe away a tear.

"Hanna," she addresses me, "when Diana died I blamed you. I thought you had something to do with it. Somehow it all just didn't seem right. Not until the constable came by and explained everything to us did I realize that not only were you not guilty, but you were the person who believed in her the most and wanted to get to the bottom of what happened to her. I will be forever grateful for that. We all will." She turns to Mr. Turner and Jeffrey, who both nod in agreement. "So we've come by to tell you how sorry we are that we ever suspected you."

I look at her in amazement. She is so contrite I am speechless. My mother steps in. "Hanna loved your daughter. They were best friends. I don't know what it is like to lose a child but it must be unbearable, and if you act a little peculiar or suspect things, well, I think it's not that surprising. So don't you feel bad." My mother pats her hand.

"Yes," I say, "I don't blame you one bit, and I'm very glad the truth has come out and you know all about it, and no matter what, I will always think of Diana as my best friend."

The group has grown quiet and solemn and my mother gets up to pour tea.

"Now please have some tea and cookies. Grace and Ida baked these." My mother is trying to be lighter and bring the conversation to a happier level.

We all sit for a minute sipping tea, and then Mrs. Turner speaks again. "You know all this might not have happened if she wasn't so much like me." She takes another sip as we all wait to hear why she thinks this is true. "I'm an animal lover, and I instilled that into Diana. She hated to see an animal injured or someone be cruel to an animal. We had a steady procession of animals at our house, really more than we could feed, but somehow she always managed to provide for them. It was just this last one. That damned raccoon. She didn't tell us she had it. Maybe if she had we could have stopped the whole affair. She should have known better. She knew about rabies. She was probably afraid that if she told us the animal would have to be killed. You know that's what they do to determine if the animal has rabies. They look at its brain under a microscope. She's had so many animals. Lots of them died – you can't save them all. She had a little baby squirrel once. She kept it in a pouch pinned to her blouse to keep it warm and she'd use an eyedropper to feed it every couple of hours. That little thing lived. And it wasn't just the furry things she liked. She loved frogs and turtles and even snakes, bugs, birds, you name it." Mrs. Turner paused. "Sorry I'm rattling on. She was so sweet. I miss her so." She sniffs and wipes her eye again. We all sip our tea.

Mrs. Turner goes on. "Well, we were thinking that maybe we could do something to remember her by, maybe a little science scholarship at the school. We talked to Mr. Anders about it and he thought it was a good idea and he was planning how to do it, to get contributions from the community to fund it. We'd call it the Diana Turner Biology Scholarship. What do you think?"

"I think that is a wonderful idea." My mother is the first to respond. We all agree.

"The pastor said he would even talk about it in church. He would help fundraise, maybe even have church dinners to help. Everyone has been so kind and wants to lend a hand." She sips her tea. "Even some of the ladies I work for want to contribute. I think once the stigma of suicide was erased people have been much kinder to us." She looks at me. "You know, it is all due to your efforts." I smile.

Mr. Turner watches intently. He nods with a strange little bounce as his wife talks about Diana and about the scholarship. Finally he speaks. "You have been a good friend, Hanna, and your family has been good to us. We will always remember your kindness." He looks down at the hat in his hand as a tear splatters onto it. He rises and steps back but remains in the room.

Although I never look directly at Jeffrey, I see him sitting silently all the while, looking dejected as he follows the conversation and nods at the appropriate moments. He is polite and neat. His hair is clean and combed, his face shaved and his shirt pressed. He looks more presentable than I have ever seen him look. And when he finally speaks I am surprised at how thoughtfully he chooses his words.

"Hanna, I told my parents about the day you came by to get Diana's diary. I am ashamed to have acted the way I did. You are a respectable girl and I should never have treated you with such disrespect. I have no excuse for doing so. I am very, very sorry. I will never do anything like that again." His gaze drops to his hands.

My mother looks from him to me, not fully knowing what exactly went on that day.

"Jeffrey, thank you. I accept your apology." Then he lifts his eyes and we smile at each other.

My mother, baffled, again looks from one of us to the other. Mr. and Mrs. Turner smile.

"Well, let's have some more tea. Can you stay for dinner?" My mother is happy to share her abundance.

Chapter 41 – Jacob

We get word that Jacob spent his last days in the hospital under heavy sedation. Although they started the rabies serum series on him he had been exposed for too long for it to be effective, and he passed about a week after his crazy display at the school.

I feel bad for him. He really tried to take care of Diana. He was the only Sparks who tried to do the right thing. She had that prince she never thought she'd have and he was true to her until the end.

We all attend the service, everyone in town. Mr. and Mrs. Sparks are in black, as are their two sons. There is no coffin; Jacob was cremated by order of town cemetery officials, who said burying his body was just too dangerous. When the family enters the church and we all turn to see the procession of pallbearers we find only an urn, carried by Edmund, followed by Gilbert junior with his head bowed, and then the parents. She leans heavily on his arm and he bends towards her. I have never seen the two of them look so deflated. He doesn't have that arrogant chest-out stance he usually sports. He doesn't carry his head high. His hair, normally washed and glistening black, is greasy and uncombed. He failed in his effort to break his son, and his failure broke him.

I see familiar faces. Silver-haired Dr. Hunt, accompanied by his wife, looks professional with grey fedora in hand, his other hand holding his wife's grey-gloved one. Turning my head I see the constable, looking sharp in his uniform, with his tiny little wife on his arm. Then I see Pastor Clark trying to be unassuming in a church that he doesn't lead, holding his wife's hand. Mr. Anders is there with his sweet wife, both looking very sad.

Unexpectedly the doctor gets up to speak, saying how sad he is and everyone should be over this unnecessary loss. He talks about rabies and how we all must be cautious and aware that a wild animal's bite can kill and to always tell someone if we are bitten. I think the congregation is surprised by this but the doctor seems satisfied he has done all he can to protect his community.

The service is similar to Diana's. The pastor talks of the fine boy the community has lost. Then he speaks words of comfort to assure everyone that a good boy like Jacob will certainly find peace with Jesus and His Father in heaven.

As we all follow the family out of the church I notice that tucked in the corner of the back row are the Turners. Their daughter's funeral is not long past and another sad event has followed on its heels. We all file down the steps to the road on a journey much like the one we made less than six months ago. Today, though, the sun is shining, the birds are singing, and it is spring. The earth smells rich and ripe and the spring flowers send their aromas wafting into the warm air. I can't help but reflect on how different this is from Diana's sad journey and I remember how she once wrote in her diary that she wanted to die in the springtime. Did she have a premonition her life would be short? On such a beautiful morning I think she is right; it does seem like a good time to die.

We shuffle along the road, and finally reaching the cemetery we see a large plot staked out but only a tiny hole in which to place the urn holding Jacob's ashes. Behind the small hole lie a number of unassembled granite slabs, which look like the pieces of a large cemetery monument. His father is assuaging his guilt by building a grand monument to his youngest son. The sight of it makes me sadder than just a small headstone would have. If only his father had given Jacob the love and respect in life that he now seems to want to bestow upon him in death. How pitiful.

While we all stand at the gravesite and listen to the pastor pray over the urn, Cecil flies to a nearby branch and adds his cawing to the prayers. Jeffrey tries to shoo him away but Cecil stays and quiets down after a minute or two.

We are all invited back to the church hall, where a large buffet has been laid out. But on the way, rather than go to the hall the Sparkses climb slowly up the granite steps to their fine house on the hill. A quiet falls upon the crowd gazing at them. Without a word we watch the family enter their home.

My father, who hadn't heard about Gilbert senior's cheating on his wife, says he was never the same after that. He withdrew from politics and was even a kinder employer, helping those who had difficulties and promoting those he thought deserved it. When his son Gilbert junior got into trouble again he let him take the consequences, hoping, we all supposed, that he would finally learn a lesson if his father wasn't there to bail him out. And when we saw Marie Sparks at the market, she was sometimes even smiling.

Chapter 42 - What Followed

The whole town was changed by the events of that fall and spring, and it will be a long time before those years are forgotten.

I did go to college and will soon graduate close to the top of my class. Constable Cruthers is still my mentor and says I can probably get a job as an assistant in his office when I graduate.

Dr. Hunt stayed in the village and is there still. We see him and his wife walking arm in arm to the post office and back. He's looking for a replacement he can train to take over his practice, but so far no one has met his standards.

Mr. Anders still teaches and champions the scholarship that he started with the Turners. He is always looking for young scientists to inspire.

Pastor Clark still gives sermons that keep us awake. He encourages the young people who stop in and debate with him. He says they keep him fresh and up with the times.

Mr. Turner told us Gilbert senior became a much kinder boss and that changed the whole dynamic at the mill. He said he found it a better place to work and he did a better job and has even gotten a promotion. He's doing work that allows him to make the most use of his good arm and that is unaffected by the lost use of the other.

Mrs. Turner still works in the village. Her employers have been kind to her and help her fund and promote the scholarship.

Gilbert junior left not only the town but also the state. We've heard that after making a name for himself in the financial world he was jailed for embezzlement.

Grace married a farmer not far away and already has two children. Their farm is thriving and they are looking to buy adjacent property and expand.

My mother and father love having their grandchildren visit and help at their farm. They think that one day these young farmers might inherit it.

Jeffrey, after working hard at the mill for several years, opened up a little garage to fix cars. He's doing well. We stay in touch and he said he's been dating a local girl he plans to wed next year.

Harry died a few years back and they buried him in the backyard where he used to sit and wait for Diana to take him for a walk by the river.

Cecil lives with Jeffrey, next to the garage. Sitting in the tree overhead he announces loudly anyone who drives in. Mrs. Turner says he still shows up at their house occasionally and caws until she gives him a treat.

The pool on the Natchaug River became known as Diana's Pool. Kids still crowd around it on warm summer days and fishermen line its shore on cool spring days. And I will always remember my best friend who loved her animals and the woods that line the shores of the pool.

Afterword

My attempts to research the legend of Diana's Pool to discover the origin of the name yielded no concrete information but three possible theories: It was named as in the story, after a girl called Diana, who threw herself into the pool when a lover spurned her; or a family named Diana owned the property and may or may not have had a small concession business there; or, according to Rusty Lanzit, some "highfalutin" kids from Hampton named it after the goddess Diana.

If by chance anyone has information about the real story behind Diana's Pool, I would be happy to put it on my web page and give the credit where it is due.

The historic district of Chaplin is a historian's dream. Many of the houses there originate from around 1815 when the town was built up very quickly. The road through the historic village was bypassed when the state highway, Route 198, was constructed, helping to keep the integrity of the village intact.

Chaplin had a church, school, town hall, library, post office, store and tavern. A drive along its main street gives one the feeling of how the village looked 150 years ago.

Although I used the buildings in Chaplin as a backdrop for the story, the story itself is fictional. Any resemblance to actual persons living or dead, or resemblance to actual events, is purely coincidental.

Diana K. Perkins

Dianas Pool, Chaplin, Conn.

Shetucket River Milltown Series

Other novels by Diana K. Perkins set in Eastern Connecticut:

Singing Her Alive, set in Willimantic, is a love story centering on two time periods, presented as a fictional memoir. The primary story begins in the late 1800s when fate throws two young women together as boardinghouse roommates - in a shared bed - at a textile mill where they have gone to work, far from home and family. Two generations later their secrets comes to light when a granddaughter, narrator of the story, finds their personal journals hidden in a closet as she helps her mother clean out their family homestead to sell. The discovery of these family secrets sets the narrator on her own journey towards identity and place. Love and sacrifice, choices and consequences, are strong themes in this story. It has received five-star reviews on Amazon and very good reviews on GoodReads, Barnes and Noble, and other websites.

Jenny's Way, based on a local legend, is a fictional tale set in Baltic, Connecticut. The story spans four decades, from the 1930s to the 1960s. It follows the entwined lives of three families, each with its own destiny, weaving together their dark and light threads throughout the years. These families create a tapestry of local color: a good hardworking farm family, a family with difficulties, and an extended family of women who are supported by the kindnesses of the mill boys they service. *Jenny's Way* has won first place in the historical fiction category of the Next Generation Indie Book Awards.

http://dianakperkins.com

Made in the USA
Charleston, SC
22 November 2014